SHANKS ON CRIME

by

Robert Lopresti

Shanks on Crime
Copyright ©2003–2014 Robert Lopresti

Published by Robert Lopresti

ebook ISBN: 978-0-9904784-0-9
print ISBN: 978-0-9904784-1-6

Library of Congress control number: 2014946248.

www.RobLopresti.com

Cover photo by Lorrie B. Potters.
Back cover photo by Crista Dougherty.

Book design, prepress, and ebook design by Kate Weisel, weiselcreative.com

"Shanks at Lunch" first appeared in *Alfred Hitchcock's Mystery Magazine,* February 2003.

"Shanks Goes Hollywood" first appeared in *Alfred Hitchcock's Mystery Magazine,* April 2005.

"Shanks Gets Mugged" first appeared in *Alfred Hitchcock's Mystery Magazine,* December 2005.

"Shanks on the Prowl" first appeared in *Alfred Hitchcock's Mystery Magazine,* May 2006.

"Shanks Gets Killed" first appeared in *Alfred Hitchcock's Mystery Magazine,* May 2009.

"Shanks on Misdirection" first appeared in *Alfred Hitchcock's Mystery Magazine,* July/August 2009.

"Shanks Commences" first appeared in *Alfred Hitchcock's Mystery Magazine,* May 2012.

"Shanks Holds The Line" first appeared on *Trace Evidence,* the blog of *Alfred Hitchcock's Mystery Magazine,* May 5, 2014.

Dedicated to Cathleen Jordan,
Shanks' first friend,
and Linda Landrigan,
his best friend.

Contents

Introduction. vii

Shanks At Lunch 1

Shanks At The Bar 9

Shanks Goes Hollywood 21

Shanks Gets Mugged 34

Shanks On The Prowl 49

~ First Interlude ~ 61

Misery Loves Strange Bedfellows 62

Shanks Gets Killed 64

Shanks On Misdirection 88

Shanks' Ghost Story. 97

Shanks' Mare 106

Shanks For The Memory 122

~ Second Interlude ~ 129

Prologue For A Shanks Novel In Case I Ever Write One 130

Shanks Commences. 132

Shanks' Ride. 153

Shanks Holds The Line 162

About The Author 167

INTRODUCTION

It began in a coffeehouse in Montclair, New Jersey. I didn't meet Leopold Longshanks there, but you might say I first heard a rumor about him, got a hint that such a man existed. It took more than a decade to track him down, putting the clues together one at a time.

He seemed reluctant to come forward. Some fictional characters are like that. But once I managed to get him into a story Shanks has generally seemed eager to cooperate, to reveal more elements of his personality. Let's face it: the man has an ego.

You might say that is something he has in common with his creator. You would probably be right. (But as I note many pages from here, we are not identical. Shanks and I have very different tastes in music, booze, and exercise, just for starters. Also, he is regrettably much more successful than I am.)

This book contains all nine of Shanks' public appearances since 2003, all in ALFRED HITCHCOCK'S MYSTERY MAGAZINE (or a reasonable facsimile thereof), plus four that are appearing here for the first time. As a bonus I am including two pieces about Shanks that appeared in my blog. And, just because I like you, I have included author's notes after each story.

(Why an afterword for each story, rather than as an introduction? This way I don't have to be coy and avoid spoilers. Of course, if you are the sort of person who reads the last chapter first, feel free to flip to the end. Whatever lights your pumpkin.)

But I have taken too much of your time. You bought this volume to encounter Shanks, not me. Enjoy.

~ Robert Lopresti
March 2014

SHANKS AT LUNCH

"For heaven's sake, Shanks, try to behave yourself today."

Leopold Longshanks looked at his wife with one raised eyebrow. "Behave myself how, dear?"

Cora was frowning at the traffic light, tapping a foot as if DON'T WALK had been holding them up for hours instead of seconds. They had plenty of time to walk for two blocks, but Shanks was wise enough not to say so.

"What was that?" asked Cora.

"Is there some particular behavior you wish me to avoid?"

"Don't monopolize the conversation."

"No monopoly. Got it."

"And don't just sit there like a lump."

"No lumps. Right." The light changed and they marched forward. Shanks reflected that so far he could get in trouble by talking too much or by talking too little. Sounded like a fun afternoon.

Poor Cora. She wasn't usually like this, but she was approaching her first press interview with all the enthusiasm of a prisoner marching to the gallows.

"You know," Shanks said cautiously – he didn't want her to think he was attempting to desert – "if you don't want me to be there at all, I could meet you after—"

"No. You better come along. I suppose that if the questions get too tough I can draw on your vast experience."

Standard sarcasm, but delivered too quickly. Twenty-plus years of marriage had taught Shanks to spot a white lie as soon as it raised its nervous little head. In this case, he suspected Cora had had to promise his presence to clinch the interview.

That was too bad, she deserved better. But Shanks had been a writer for too long to expect the publishing business to be fair.

As they reached the tea shop, Cora saw herself in the front window and dug up a brand-new worry. "I should have worn the green dress. I look like a sack of potatoes in this thing."

Ah. He knew the proper response for that one. "You look terrific in that outfit."

"But I look better in the green—"

"True."

"True?" She spun around to stare at him, as if he had proclaimed that she looked elderly. *And* six months pregnant.

"But you don't want to show up this lady reporter too much, do you? I mean, in this outfit there's a chance she won't be totally outclassed."

Cora grinned and looked a little more like herself. "Flatterer."

They had just gotten settled into a table by the tea shop's front window when their guest arrived. Shanks was a fair judge of interviewers, and by the time Rose Marotta had shaken hands he had classified her as a Modified Gusher (magazine variety), given to limp questions and inaccurate quotations. If anyone had been there to take a bet he would have offered three-to-one odds that she would ask the Worst Question.

"What a pleasure to meet you—" she bubbled. "The wife of such a famous author! And you, Leopold Longshanks! I've been reading your books since I was a child!" And having offended both of her subjects, she sat blithely down to dine with them.

"Mr. Longshanks, I want—"

"Call me Shanks. Everyone does." That got him a kick under the table. Apparently he was already talking too much. After they ordered depressingly dainty sandwiches – he would need a steak when he got home – he took the gamble of saying more. "I am so glad you want to interview Cora about her wonderful first novel."

"Oh, absolutely," Rose said, blinking a lot, as if suddenly remembering why she was there. "So tell me, Cora, what is it like now that there are *two* novelists in the house?"

Well, that was nearly on topic, anyway. While his wife gave a sparklingly fresh, carefully rehearsed answer to that, Shanks gazed out the window – they had arranged for the two women to face each other, with the odd man out sitting between them.

He frowned. There was a bench in front of the bank across the street and someone had left a black bundle under one end. It looked about the right size and shape for a laptop computer in a leather case.

He had been looking for a good opening for an Inspector Cadogan novel about terrorism. A bomb left at a bus stop? Too much of a cliché, perhaps.

Rose was asking Cora if he had given her any advice about writing. Shanks had warned his wife that the reporter would either write that he had been her loving mentor, guiding her progress toward authorship, or else that she had nobly put off her writing for all these years to support him. That Cora had developed an interest in writing on her own a few years ago and worked at her craft more or less independently did not fit any of the current myths, so he knew the reporter would shoehorn her into the role of either lucky pupil or self-sacrificing spouse. The best Cora could hope for was being permitted to select which cliché would be applied to her.

A middle-aged man with a tan sports coat and bow tie sat down at the end of the bench farthest from the bundle and opened a newspaper. Immediately a younger man in a red nylon jacket came over and sat down end of the bench. He spotted the bundle and said something to the other man.

Is this yours? Shanks guessed.

Bow Tie shook his head and went back to his newspaper. Redcoat picked up the bundle.

And Cora kicked him again. He had missed a question. "Rose was saying, darling." Cora muttered through gritted teeth, "How much she enjoyed your books about Tom and Tina Shaw."

"You write so well about women," said the reporter, "I was wondering if Tina is based on your lovely wife."

"Well," said Shanks. "Everything I know about women I learned from Cora. That's why I am so glad she has written a novel, so that everyone else can learn from her, too."

Which steered the conversation away from him for awhile. Across the street Redcoat had opened the bundle – it *was* a laptop computer – and was fiddling with it. He said something to Bow Tie, who reluctantly slid down the bench to help.

"I don't consider it a romance novel," Cora was saying with a chill in her voice. "If you must have a label, women's fiction is more accurate."

"Oh, I love women authors," said Rose. "Grafton, Paretsky, Christie, Sayers…"

Shanks wondered whether the interviewer had known in advance that Cora had *not* written a mystery.

The two men on the bench were very excited about something on the computer screen. From the furtive glances they cast around the street and the way they leaned together to speak, it must have been something they weren't supposed to see. My, my. What was *that* all about?

Shanks frowned. It all seemed vaguely familiar, like a scene he had read once, or even one he had written.

A man in a black coat came into view at the left edge of the shop window. He halted for a moment and then started forward toward the men on the bench.

Shanks sat up straight. In the moment his peripheral vision caught that little hesitation – the man in black assessing the scene before marching in – he realized what he was watching. The Pigeon Drop! The oldest short con in the history of confidence games.

He had read all about it while researching *Clothesline,* the novel that had won him his first Edgar. In the end he had rejected the Pigeon Drop as too old and corny to be believable, and yet here it was, large as life, on the streets of Madison.

The con men had simply modernized it by using a laptop computer instead of a wallet. Nothing odd about that, he reflected. On the streets of Caesar's Rome they probably did it with bags of gold. What was the Latin for "never give the sucker an even break?"

The man in the black coat and gray fedora had overheard the two me on the bench and force his way into the conversation. Now they were telling him, reluctantly, what they had found on the computer.

What was that, Shanks wondered. Swiss bank account numbers? A stock market tip? Something that required immediate cash and promised an immediate, if illegal, gain. Preferably, the supposed loser of the money would be an anonymous corporation or, better yet, someone it would be a downright public service to rob. A software billionaire, say.

He desperately wanted to tell Cora about what he was seeing, but that would be a mistake. Rose's article would be all about Leopold Longshanks solving a real-life crime and Cora Neal's novel would be a footnote. Grounds for divorce in any state.

The three men were making their plans now, heads together for conspiratorial whispers. *I know how to get at that money! But I need some cash to pay someone off.*

Or open an account. Or any of a dozen excuses.

Fedora was tapping rapidly at the computer Redcoat was pulling out his wallet. And Bow Tie, with an excited nod, was heading for the bank. To draw out his life savings, no doubt.

The two con men watched him go. Fedora said something that made Redcoat laugh.

Rose, meanwhile, was asking the Worst Question. "So tell me, Cora, where do you get your ideas?"

Shanks had prepped his wife for that one, and she steered firmly away from the meaningless generalities that made so many authors look like mystics or morons. "Well, the idea for this book came from an article I read two years ago about a dating service for people with severe phobias..."

Shanks' fingers itched to whisk out his cell phone. Call the police and... No. Cora would accuse him of grandstanding, of ruining her first interview.

"Excuse me," he said. "Need the restroom." His wife looked as if he was deserting her in her hour of need but that couldn't be helped.

He found a pay phone at the back of the restaurant and dialed 911. Cell phone calls, after all, could be traced. "There's a robbery going on on Blake Avenue, between Third and Fourth, in front of the bank. No, not a bank robbery. In *front* of the bank." He described the victim and the two conspirators. "It's happening even as we speak, so get over here. My name? Miles Archer."

He returned to the table. Bow Tie had also come back and was giving

Redcoat a fat envelope, full of cash no doubt. In order to count the money Redcoat handed the laptop over to Fedora.

Oh, that was good. Shanks was watching for it and yet he barely saw it. Fedora had slipped the black case under his black coat for just a moment and pulled it back out.

But it wasn't the same case now. The working computer was tucked under the trench coat. The black leather case he handed to Bow Tie held a junker, or maybe something else that weighed about the same.

Redcoat was done counting Bow Tie's money. He handed it back to Fedora with his own, and Fedora marched off, supposedly to a bank or a broker, or whatever the scam called for. Redcoat and Bow Tie stood, watching him go talking excitedly.

Rose asked Shanks to autograph one of his paperbacks. "For my little nephew. He just loves your books." Reporters were so selfless; they always wanted autographs for someone else.

Across the street, Redcoat was getting antsy. He did a good imitation of a man in need of a restroom. Finally he turned urgently to Bow Tie, and Shanks guessed what he was saying. *I'll be right back. Promise me you won't move an inch! You've got the computer. We're trusting you!* Then he walked off briskly in the opposite direction of the one Fedora had taken.

And then there was one. Shanks was fascinated. When would Bow Tie get suspicious enough to peek in the case and discover that he wasn't holding the computer with the secret formula, or Swiss bank account numbers, or whatever he thought he had seen?

The bland lunch and equally bland interview were rolling to an end. Cora smiled as she handed Rose another copy of the packet of information on her novel, Shanks had warned her never to underestimate a reporter's ability to lose P.R. material.

Outside, a police car came rolling up. Shanks was interested to see a cop open a back door and let Redcoat out of the back. No handcuffs, so he wasn't under arrest, but he certainly wouldn't have come along willingly. That probably meant he had acted suspiciously when the cops spotted him, so they had decided to hold onto him while they checked things out.

Now Bow Tie was being questioned by a cop. He looked guilty as hell and very confused. After all, he thought he was part of a conspiracy to rob the owner of the computer. But the cop had been told *he* was the victim of a robbery. Quite a puzzle.

"Time to go," said Cora.

Shanks paid the bill and the three of them stepped out into the daylight as Bow Tie opened the computer case and a couple of bricks fell out. No computer. After a moment of shock Bow Tie decided he would be happy to cooperate with the police, mostly by screaming things at Redcoat at the top of his lungs.

The three lunch companions stopped for a moment to watch the scene across the street. "What do you think that is all about?" Cora asked.

"Who knows?" he said.

Rose smiled. "Could this inspire your next mystery, Shanks?"

He shrugged. "Reality is overrated as a muse. Imagination leads to fewer libel suits."

The reporter laughed and waved goodbye.

Cora let out a breath. "How do you think it went?"

Shanks tried to look judicious. "Pretty well, I think. Your answers were better than her questions, but you can't help that."

And, just to make it perfect, here came a second police car with Fedora. Not a good day for the flimflam boys.

Cora took his hand. "Oh, Shanks. Do you really think my book will sell well?"

"It's a damned good novel, honey. If there's any justice, it will do just fine."

His wife sighed. "Yes, but is there any justice?"

Fedora and Redcoat were being fitted for handcuffs as Shanks and his wife walked past. The two con men looked mightily ticked off. Bow Tie was still calling them imaginative but accurate names.

Shanks laughed. "Oh, sometimes there is justice, my love. Every once in a great while." And he took her hand.

As I said in the introduction, it all started in a coffee shop. My wife and I were at a table by the window with a friend. I don't know what the topic under discussion was but my mind started to drift and I found my-self wondering: What if I saw a crime outside the window? And what if, for some reason, I couldn't interrupt the conversation to do something about it?

I pondered that situation for years. I needed a nonviolent crime, be-cause a beating, for example, would demand immediate action. And then I needed the sort of character who would spot what was going on, think it through, and take appropriate action.

There's a popular idea that mainstream fiction is based in character and genre fiction is based on plot. Also, some people say that character is action and action is character. So we've got that cleared up.

But I am grateful that it took me years to work out the plot because that gave Leopold Longshanks the time to germinate. And he blossomed in the February 2003 issue of ALFRED HITCHCOCK'S MYSTERY MAGAZINE.

The more observant (or nosier) readers may be asking: if the coffee-house was in Montclair, why is this story set in Madison? Again, blame it on the length of time it took me to write the story. By then I had been away from New Jersey long enough that I mixed up the names. I real-ized it when I saw it in print, but by then it was too late.

They're both nice towns, anyway.

SHANKS AT THE BAR

Once or twice a year someone approached Leopold Longshanks and started what he thought of as The Routine.

Usually this happened at a book signing, where he was financially obligated to be polite. The customer would march up to the table where Shanks was seated, trying to look both authorial and approachable.

The customer would have a determined look on her face – it was usually a her – as she stated her name. "You probably don't remember me," she would say, "but we met last year at the mystery convention."

Shanks' response was always the same. His shoulders and bushy eyebrows would start to rise in an apologetic shrug. Then, at half-mast, so to speak, he would switch to a frown of intense concentration. At last a delighted smile would burst forth.

"Of course! It was in the bar, wasn't it?"

And the fan would be thrilled, her very existence justified by being remembered by the great author. Sometimes, wonder of wonders, she even bought one of his books.

Shanks' technique was not based on having a great memory for faces or names. It depended instead on the fact that, when he was at a mystery convention, he was almost always in the bar.

For instance, here he was at a regional convention, sitting in an oppressively cheerful, horrifyingly well-lit hotel bar, brooding over a beer. He was asking himself: who dreamed up the subjects for the panels at this thing, anyway?

Earlier that afternoon he had been on a panel called "Foxes and Lions: Young Turks Versus Elder Statesmen." Well, damn it, he was far too young to be an elder *anything*.

And look at the panel he would moderate the next day: "My Grumble

Is Quick: Kvetches From The Masters." He half-suspected that Cora had set that one up somehow. She was always complaining about the fact that he was always complaining.

"Excuse me, Mr. Longshanks?"

He looked up at a nervous man in his thirties whose name tag identified him as Ted Grider. "I hope I'm not bothering you. I just wanted to say what an honor it is to meet you. I've been reading your books for years."

At least he didn't say he had been reading them since he was a child. Shanks hated when fully-grown adults said that, as if he had been churning out one a year since Edgar Allan Poe was a rookie.

Damn. He really *did* complain about everything.

"Call me Shanks." He went on automatic pilot, nodding politely while Grider explained that he too was a mystery writer, as yet unpublished. Shanks cast a surreptitious look around. The young man hadn't been carrying a manuscript, had he? He sincerely hoped that Grider was not looking for a free edit, or worse, a recommendation to Shanks' agent.

But it seemed that Grider was looking for something less material than that. He explained that the only publisher who had bothered to give a reason for rejecting his novel had said it was humdrum. Nothing unique, nothing to make it stand out from the pack.

"What I need," Grider explained, "is a gimmick."

Shanks squinted. "A gimmick?"

"You know, something different. A cat that solves crimes. A hero who *hides* criminals instead of finding them. An Indian shaman."

"Those have all been used."

"Exactly." Grider nodded enthusiastically. "I need a *new* one. All the successful writers have one."

"What's mine?"

"Excuse me?"

"What's *my* gimmick, exactly?" asked Shanks. He was genuinely interested.

Grider looked thoughtful. "Well, your policeman is sort of—" He frowned. "You don't really have one."

"Damn."

"Of course, it was easier to get along without one in *your* day. Back in the Golden Age—"

Shanks nearly spilled his beer. "Now, hold on! I wasn't even *born* during the so-called Golden Age."

"Oh, I didn't mean it like that. Gosh, I—"

"*There* you are!" The merciful interruption came from Cora, entering the bar with a couple of friends. "Who are you boring now, Shanks?"

He introduced Grider to the newcomers. "My wife, Cora Neal. And these are Megan McKenzie and Ross Perry."

The would-be writer was suitable impressed. "Wow, I've read all your stuff," he told Megan and Ross. And then to Cora: "Uh, do you write under your own name?"

She smiled sweetly. "Meaning you've never heard of me. Yes, I do, dear, but I write mainstream fiction. Not mysteries like all these hacks."

"So you don't bother with a plot," said Ross. "Big deal."

Cora chose to ignore him. "Megan and I were watching a panel on women in peril."

"The old standby," said Megan. As a writer of romantic suspense she had created more books than even Shanks, and was a bit of an old standby herself. "And we picked up Ross here at the end of his book-signing stint."

"It should have been over a long time ago," said Ross, "but there was a big crowd and I hate to turn them away. They were so excited by the chance to meet me."

Ross's latest spy novel was nominated for an award that would be given out at this convention. Shanks wondered whether he himself was as obnoxious as Ross when *he* was up for an award. Probably.

"Has Nick shown up yet?" Megan asked. Her husband was not part of the mystery community and usually headed for the nearest golf course as soon as they reached a convention hotel.

Shanks shook his head. "Have you ladies decided where we're going for dinner?"

"Not quite," said Cora. "But I've read about a great vegetarian restaurant downtown."

"Hmm," said Shanks, poker-faced. If he protested that would just make her more determined to smother him in carrots and eggplant.

"Hey," Ross said, looking concerned. "You don't want to travel *too* far. You might miss the awards ceremony."

"Good point," said Shanks. "You know, I hear there's a fine restaurant, right here in the hotel. It happens to be a steak house, but it's very convenient."

"Hmm," said Cora, who knew his every trick. "Maybe we'll let Nick decide."

Shanks shrugged. Now his dinner would depend on Nick's golf game. If Nick did well he would want to celebrate with something full of blood and cholesterol. If he did poorly he would atone with health food.

Shanks said a silent prayer for birdies and eagles.

"It's such an honor to be sitting here with all these writers," said Ted Grider. "Can I buy you a drink?"

They graciously assented. When the libations arrived Grider spoke again. "Something I wanted to ask. Have any of you ever tried to solve a real crime?"

Cora laughed. "These clowns? They can't even change the oil in their cars. Shanks—" She patted her husband's hand. "Can barely find his shoes in the morning."

He scowled. "Even if that canard were true, what would it have to do with my ability to solve a crime?"

"My books aren't really about crime-solving, per se," said Ross, gliding into Interview Mode. "They are adventure stories, of course, and social commentary. Take *Blood Jockeys,* for example, which happens to be nominated for—"

"We know," said Megan. "Everyone knows. But seriously, Ted, mystery writers are notoriously bad at solving true crimes. Our imaginations run away with us. Of course, Conan Doyle had some success—"

"Not so," Shanks growled. "He didn't *solve* crimes. He just pointed out flaws in the police case against some defendants. That's not being a detective *or* a writer. That's just being a *critic.*" He said the word with distaste.

"Why do you ask, Ted?" said Cora.

The young man shrugged. "I was just thinking about a real mystery that happened in my family. It made me wonder if you people could shed any light on it. But I don't want to impose—"

"Oh, now we have to hear it," said Megan. "Do tell." The others, halfway through their donated drinks, nodded consent.

Grider took a deep breath. "Well, this happened a long time ago. Let's see. My cousin Carl was born in early 1954, so this would have been in the summer of 1953. My mother's family lived in Queens, New York, and her older sister Pearl was Carl's mother.

"Aunt Pearl was a nurse at a hospital in Washington, D.C. She had married Uncle Glen that spring. It was a sudden thing – he was just getting out of the Navy when they met. Over the summer they drove up north so he could meet her family."

Grider sipped beer. "They drove straight up the Garden State Parkway, but just above Red Bank there was a terrible accident."

"What happened?" asked Cora.

"Two cars collided in front of them, side by side, and went flying off the road in opposite directions. Uncle Glen managed to stop their car safely and Aunt Pearl ran out to help the victims. She was a nurse, remember."

"Was everyone all right?" asked Megan.

"The man who was driving one of the cars had been thrown out and killed. This was long before seatbelts, of course. The passenger, another man, wasn't badly hurt. The only person in the other car was a woman and she had a broken leg and a broken nose. Aunt Pearl spent almost half an hour taking care of them until the ambulance arrived."

"So what's the mystery?" asked Ross. "The cause of the accident?"

"No. It was pretty clear that the male driver had been drinking. The mystery was Uncle Glen."

"What about him?" asked Shanks.

"He disappeared." Grider held up his open hands to show the absence of uncles. "Aunt Pearl never saw him again after she left of the car."

Megan rubbed her hands together. "Oh, that's a *good* one. Did she report it to the police?"

"Of course. They showed up for the accident, of course. They looked all over, and found nothing."

"Hospitals," said Shanks. "Maybe he went in with the victims."

"They checked," said Grider. "No luck."

"Was he in his Navy uniform?" asked Ross.

"No. He had left the service just before they married."

"Did they have to stop the car very suddenly?" asked Megan.

"I have no idea," said Grider. "Why do you ask?"

"I think they did," said Megan. "I think your Uncle Glen slammed on the brakes and banged his head against the windshield."

"Then what?" asked Cora. "They bandaged his head so much that his own wife didn't recognize him?"

"Not at all," said Megan, with a satisfied smile. "He was suffering from amnesia."

"Oh, *please,*" Shanks said.

"It's obvious," Megan went on. "He bumped his head when the car slammed to a halt. Pearl ran out to help the injured people but had no idea her own husband was hurt." She gazed off as if she could see it all, somewhere behind the bartender. "He climbed out of the car and stumbled away from the scene. Someone else picked him up and whisked him off to a *different* hospital. *That's* what happened."

"Nobody has amnesia for forty years," said Shanks. "He would have long since recovered."

Megan nodded earnestly. "That's the tragic part. By the time he recovered he had fallen in love with someone else. Perhaps a nurse at the hospital where he was treated. And he wouldn't even have known why he was attracted to a nurse."

"Then he would have had to choose between them," said Cora. Shanks saw with amazement that she seemed to be buying this theory.

"Exactly," said Megan. "But by then Pearl no doubt thought he was dead. Maybe she had found someone else—"

"She didn't," said Grider. "She raised my cousin Dave alone."

"When was Dave born?" asked Cora.

"Six months after Uncle Glen disappeared."

"I don't buy any of this," said Ross. "Amnesia is a romance novelist's trick. It hardly ever happens in real life, and when it does it's more likely to last a day than a year."

Megan gave him a sour look. "Then what's *your* explanation, Mr. Nominee?"

"Easy." Ross smiled and sipped martini. "Uncle Glen was a Navy man stationed in Washington, D.C. Right?"

"Right," said Grider.

"So chances are he either worked at the White House or across the river at the Pentagon."

"I don't know," said Grider. "Aunt Pearl never said."

Ross looked thoughtful. "1953. The Korean War was just over. I'm guessing Uncle Glen knew some military secrets. Probably about nuclear submarines, since he was in the Navy."

"So what happened?" asked Cora. "He radiated out of existence?"

"Very funny. No, he was kidnapped. The accident was no accident."

"Ah, clever," said Shanks, admiringly.

"But one driver died," said Cora. "Are you saying it was a suicide mission?"

"Very possibly. Or maybe the woman driver who survived was the one who set it up."

"Or maybe," said Shanks, getting into the spirit of the thing, "the driver was just *pretending* to be dead."

"And what was the point of this?" asked Megan, irritably.

"To create a diversion and kidnap a Navy man with valuable information." Ross nodded solemnly. "Your Uncle Glen probably spent the rest of his life in a Soviet prison."

"Wow," said Grider, wide-eyed. ""You think so?"

"Spy novel fantasy," grumbled Megan.

Ross scowled. "As opposed to the grim realism of a forty-year amnesia case?"

"What about you, Cora?" Shanks asked. "Do you have a theory?"

His wife smiled. "I do, actually. I don't know if you'll like it much, Ted."

"Fire away," said Grider.

Cora sipped wine. "Okay. Uncle Glen didn't disappear because he didn't exist."

The younger man frowned. *"Somebody* was Dave's father."

"Sure. But that doesn't necessarily mean Aunt Pearl had a husband."

"I get it," said Megan. "She found herself pregnant and unmarried. Not a good thing to be in 1953."

"Right," said Cora. "So she tells her parents she is married to a sailor. They didn't get to meet him because he was off at sea. But eventually she ran out of excuses. On the trip north—" She paused. "Are we sure the accident really happened, Ted?"

Grider nodded. "I've seen the newspaper clippings."

"Okay," said Cora. "Here's what happened. Pearl was heading north alone. Maybe she was going to tell her parents the truth. Or maybe she had a new excuse ready. But the accident gave her an idea. A foolproof way out."

"I like that one," said Megan.

Ross snorted. "I tell you, that accident was no accident. It was a *snatch.* What do you think, Shanks?"

"Me?" Shanks raised his eyebrows. "Actually, I like Cora's explanation." He glared at Ross, who had muttered something that sounded very much like *U* "But if I have to defend Aunt Pearl's honor, so to speak…"

He paused to dream up and discard a couple of suggestions. "Ah, got it. Beams falling."

"Come again?" said Grider.

"In one of Dashiell Hammett's books he wrote about an average guy, an office worker, who went out to lunch one day and was almost killed by a beam that fell off a crane at a construction site."

Shanks finished a beer and waved for another. "The fellow couldn't go back to work after receiving this *memento mori,* so to speak. Instead he boarded a train and started life over in a new city."

Grider blinked. "And how does this apply to Uncle Glen?"

"The car accident was Glen's falling beam. Your uncle said 'that could have been me.' And suddenly his life ahead seemed pitifully short and he didn't want to spend it married to this woman, meeting her parents, and so on."

Ross leapt to his feet. "Oh my gosh! Speaking of pitifully short time, I have to get ready for the banquet. You know, I've been nominated for—"

"We know," said everyone but Grider.

"We'd better get going too," said Megan. "Cora, let's go check my room. Maybe Nick went straight back there."

"Good idea." She turned to her husband. "Please try not to disappear, darling. Nice to meet you, Ted."

Once again Shanks was alone with a beer and Ted Grider. "Well, what do you think?"

"That was amazing!" The fan was wide-eyed. "Meeting all those famous writers! And I couldn't believe the way you dreamed up those theories."

"Practice. It's part of what we do for a living, after all. But what I meant was, did any of our suggestions help you with your plotting problem?"

Grider stared at him. "Come again?"

"You told me you're a writer. Obviously you're blocked and need help. So, I'm wondering if we gave you anything you can use."

The young man's shoulders sank. "What makes you think I wasn't telling the truth?"

"Well, for one thing, they were still building the Garden State Parkway in 1953. Nobody was cruising straight up it that summer."

"Damn." Grider pulled out a pen and a notebook. "I have to research that. Do you think all the writers knew I was lying?"

Shanks decided to give his colleagues the benefit of the doubt. "Oh, absolutely. But you were buying the drinks. I assume your supposed cousin Dave is your book's hero and he was traumatized by growing up without a father."

Grider stopped writing and stared at him. "Yeah. Exactly."

"So do you have your own idea about what happened to the Glen character?"

"Sure. Pearl told him she was pregnant and he decided he didn't want to be a father. He took off the next time the car stopped, and that happened to be at the accident."

Shanks nodded judiciously. "Simple and plausible, I suppose."

"Well, *I* thought so. I was surprised none of you writers thought of it."

"Oh, they may have. *I* did. But the problem with your explanation is that it's dull. No professional writer is going to offer a boring story line just because it's *plausible*."

Grider threw his notebook on the table. "But that's just it! How do you come up with a plot that's both believable *and* surprising?"

Unexpectedly, Shanks grinned. "You figure out how to do that consistently, Ted, and you won't need any other gimmick."

The elevator at the far end of the lobby opened its doors and Cora appeared. She had the determined look of a woman hunting for an errant husband.

"I'm never going to be a writer," grumbled Grider.

"Maybe it's not your line," Shanks agreed. "How about becoming a thief? You show some talent there."

"Thief?" Grider stared at him. "What are you talking about?"

"You used false pretenses to steal an hour of time from four experts, each of whom could have demanded a considerable consulting fee for the advice you received for the price of a few drinks. So, let's admit that there *was* a crime here."

The younger man stared at him. "I – I—"

Shanks let him dangle a moment longer. Then: "Oh, relax. It wasn't the crime of the century. Probably not even of the week." He emptied his beer mug. "Oh, by the way. I did think of a gimmick recently, but I'm far too busy with other books to use it myself. If you want it, it's all yours."

"Really?" The young man scooped up his notebook. "What is it?"

Shanks put his fingertips together in professorial style. "Ever since Poe, the mystery genre has depended on series detectives, correct? Different people commit different crimes but the hero moves on from book to book."

"Of course," said Grider, eagerly.

Cora had spotted them now. Shanks saw her turn and march their way with a determined stride.

"Now, recent times have seen the invention of a *new* type of character, the series villain. We have criminal masterminds and serial killers who battle different detectives in book after book and go on to strike again."

"Absolutely," said Grider. He was practically salivating.

"So, here's my new gimmick. I give it to you with my blessing." He leaned across the table and spoke in a confidential whisper. "Write a series in which each book has a different detective and murderer. But – and here is the twist – in each novel *the same person gets killed!*"

Grider quivered with excitement. "Wow! Nobody's done *that* before!"

"You'll be the first," Shanks agreed.

"*There* you are," said Cora, as if he had been hiding behind the bar instead of sitting just where she had left him. "I have to tear him away, Ted. Dinner time, Shanks."

"Great." He stood up. "It was a pleasure to meet you, Ted. Good luck with that book."

Grider looked puzzled. "But how could the same—"

"They're waiting for us," said Cora. She took his arm firmly and led him off.

"So where are we going?" Shanks asked.

"Nick is in a mood for steak. He broke ninety, whatever that means."

"Oh. I guess that vegetarian place will have to wait." Good Old Nick.

"What's Ted shouting about back there?" Cora asked. "'How could it be the same victim?' What is he talking about?"

"I have no idea," said Shanks.

After selling the first Shanks story to HITCHCOCK'S I was understandably eager to turn my one-shot into a series. (The second story is a sequel, the third makes it a series.)

SHANKS AT THE BAR was inspired by the many mystery conventions I have attended. I was also thinking of Tony Hillman's hilarious anecdotes about meetings with readers, such as the woman who wondered why he had changed the name of his main character from Joe Leaphorn to Jim Chee. Apparently all Navaho policemen look alike to her.

Unfortunately Cathleen Jordan, the wonderful editor of AHMM passed away unexpectedly in 2002. SHANKS AT THE BAR was the first story I sent to Linda Landrigan, the new editor. She rejected it, which made me very nervous about my future – and about that of Shanks as well.

I assume she turned it down because of its low crime content – although Shanks does his best to argue that a crime was indeed committed. (I don't know for sure why Linda rejected it, of course. Editors are not required to give a reason, and that's a good thing. Most of the time the reason would be "I thought it stank" and who would that help?)

Fortunately, things later turned out fine for Linda, Shanks, and I, but this story is making its first public appearance anywhere.

SHANKS GOES HOLLYWOOD

Leopold Longshanks did not enjoy playing the fool. He had a powerful prejudice, almost an allergy, against being made to look like an idiot.

And yet here he sat in a police station, waiting for exactly that to happen. The fact that he was 3,000 miles from home and would never see these people again should have been some comfort. It wasn't.

Shanks sighed. He ran over what he was going to say, trying to edit it into something more presentable. However much he tweaked it, his speech amounted to this: "Hello, officer. I'm a mystery writer and I'm here to tell you've arrested the wrong man for murder. Just sit back, relax, and let an amateur tell you how to do your job."

Might as well put on a clown suit to make the picture complete.

How in the world had it come to this? This morning when the newspaper revealed that Ed Godwen had been arrested for murder, Shanks had had no intention of getting involved. In fact, his first reaction had been to mutter: "It just goes to show."

"What does?" Cora had asked. She was gathering some paperwork before they left the hotel room for breakfast.

"Ed moved out to L.A., divorced Jean, married an actress, and now he's killed her. Some people just aren't *meant* to live in California."

"Sounds like sour grapes," his wife said.

Shanks' bushy eyebrows shot up. "About what? The actress?" He found the idea of marrying a woman twenty years younger than himself horrifying. What in the world would you *talk* about?

"No, dear. I meant the fact that Ed got rich writing bestsellers and Hollywood keeps beating down his door."

Well, there was that. Shanks' mystery novels weren't exactly setting sales records, and on the rare occasions Hollywood knocked on his door it did so in a timid and reluctant manner, as if it suspected it had come to the wrong address.

Shanks had met Ed at a publisher's party decades before when both were rookies in the writing game. They had been friends ever since, in spite of the fact that Shank secretly thought Ed's books were, well, *clunky*. Each one featured an unbelievable bad guy plotting to rule the world and a paper-thin hero defeating him with the help of some piece of cutting-edge technology. All of the gadgets were described with the sort of lush, adjective-filled prose you seldom saw outside of pornography. But millions of satisfied readers can't be wrong, can they?

The point was that Shanks was by no means convinced that Ed Godwen was innocent of the crime he had been arrested for. So why was he at a police station, waiting to look foolish?

Blame that on Jean Godwen, Ed's first wife, who was still very much alive. She had called that morning while driving up from San Diego – she moved there after the divorce – and invited the Longshanks family to lunch.

Cora had to beg off; she would be dining with her agent and some TV producers. She and Shanks were visiting the left coast because a cable network had come banging on the door for one of *her* novels – romance, not mystery.

And Shanks was just fine with her success, really. *Really.*

Cora had urged him to have lunch with Jean. "Maybe she'll have some good gossip about Ed."

Which she did, sort of.

"Ed didn't kill her," Jean said as soon as he sat down. Shanks looked around. Even here, in an outdoor café in Malibu, that opening line had drawn a few startled glances. "You *know* he wouldn't."

"No, I don't," he said, quietly. "I don't even know that *I* wouldn't kill someone, given the right fit of rage. And Ed has more of a temper than I do."

"Shanks, you have to find out who really killed Abitha!"

"Me?" He stared at her. "Jean, are you crazy? I don't know how to solve crimes. I just make stuff up."

"Ed says you're the smartest man he knows."

He doubted that. Doubted it was true and doubly doubted that Ed had ever said it. If he was such a genius why was he barely paying the mortgage writing genre mysteries while Ed was buying second homes with his techno-thrillers?

"A man as smart as you could figure out where the police made their mistake—"

"Which they probably did *not*," said Shanks. "When they arrest someone for murder they usually have the right guy. And when he's rich and famous they're even more careful. Besides—" He hesitated.

"Yes?" Jean's gray eyes were calm and determined. *A handsome woman,* Shanks thought. *Ed had been a fool to toss her aside.*

"When a wife gets murdered the husband is the natural suspect. Plus, he's an older man, married to a beautiful actress."

"*Exactly,*" said Jean. "The cops haven't investigated the case. They've examined their stereotypes. Ed's been *profiled.*"

"Jean, this is pointless."

She was squeezing her napkin so hard he thought the linen would tear. "You're going to do this for me, Shanks."

The threat was unmistakable. "Or else what?"

"Or else I'll tell Cora about our little fling."

Shanks' eyes went wide and then he laughed. "My God, I don't know what's more outrageous. That you would try to blackmail me or that your ammunition is so shoddy."

"Well, thanks a lot."

"No offense, Jean. You're definitely worthy of Cora's jealousy. But when you and I were an item we were both single. I hadn't even *met* Cora yet. Not exactly a scandal."

"That's true," she said, and her gray eyes were mere slits. "I suppose you told Cora about us?"

Had he? "I don't think so. Gentlemen don't discuss such things."

Jean smiled like a cat that had rid the world of one more canary. "So all the time the four of us were doing things together Cora didn't know I was your former lover. If you're sure that won't bother her – based on your *vast* understanding of women – then you're right I have no ammunition at all."

Hmm.

So that was why he was sitting in a police station waiting to meet the cop in charge of the investigation. This turned out to be a detective named Mike Cranepool, a muscular blond in his thirties who looked like he ought to be starring in cop movies, rather than living them.

Shanks figured the interview would be mercifully short. He would ask to see Ed, get told off for trying to interfere with a murder investigation, apologize, and be out in fifteen minutes. Twenty, tops. He could honestly tell Jean he had done everything he could.

"I know you aren't Mr. Godwen's lawyer," said Cranepool, "because he's already been here. Are you a relative?"

Shanks shook his head. "Just a friend. We're in the same business."

"Well, I'm sorry, Mr. Longshanks. Mr. Godwen can't see anyone today. Tomorrow he'll be moved to a central—" The cop stopped. He frowned. "Longshanks. Where have I heard that name?"

"I'm a writer," Shanks admitted.

Cranepool's face burst into a sudden smile of delight. If someone had offered Shanks a thousand guesses, he would never have been able to predict what would come next. "You wrote *Streets of Scorpio!*"

Shanks blinked. "Sort of. I didn't write the screenplay."

"That's right. You wrote the novelization."

His eyebrows dropped into a dangerous scowl. "I wrote the *novel* on which the screenplay was based. Not a novelization, which is a sort of a *shadow* of a novel, a ghost of a screenplay pretending to be—"

Oh, shut up, he told himself. *The cop doesn't care.*

Cranepool was still smiling. "I *loved* that flick. It's a classic."

Which didn't say much for his taste. *Streets of Scorpio* had been based – loosely – on one of Shanks' first novels. The geniuses at the studio had turned Inspector Cadogan – middle-aged, laconic, by turns lazy and obsessive – into a young martial arts expert whose entire personality seemed to consist of driving a sports car and swearing a lot. On the rare occasions Shanks mentioned the movie he usually called it *Straight to Video,* which was more or less what had happened to it.

"Glad you liked it."

The cop leaned back in his chair and gave Shanks a look that could only be called cunning. "I don't suppose it would do any *harm* to let you see Mr. Godwen."

Shanks jaw dropped. Could anyone be *that* fond of a bad movie?

"And if I let you do that," said the detective, "maybe you could do a favor for *me*."

Uh oh. Warning bells rang urgently in Shanks' head. The cop had a manuscript – or, this being L.A., a screenplay – and he wanted Shanks to pass it on to his own agent. Or worse, perhaps he was one of the many people who thought that writers were always desperate for ideas. *I'll tell you about all the amazing things that happened to me on the force. You do the easy part, just turn them into novels, and we'll split the money fifty-fifty!*

But Cranepool smiled enigmatically and refused to go into details. "We can discuss it after you see Mr. Godwen."

Ouch. Because only a boor would refuse to return a favor that had already been granted. Mentally, Shanks swore a terrible oath at Jean for getting him into this.

A few minutes later Cranepool led him to an interrogation room. One wall was mirrored.

"Don't touch him. Don't hand him anything or the interview is over. And you might as well assume someone is listening from behind the mirror."

Shanks had already guessed that part.

When Ed entered he was not in handcuffs, but he was wearing a bright orange prison jumpsuit. "Shanks! Jeez, is that you?"

He looked ten years older than the last time Shanks had seen him, which had not been long after the marriage to Abitha Peel, two years ago. Shanks remembered that evening well.

The actress-bride had struck him as a whiny, self-absorbed little egotist, ready to pout whenever the conversation drifted away from the subject of her wonderful self. When she discovered that Shanks and Cora had seen only one of her movies she dropped into a sulk that lasted for the entire drive to dinner. At the restaurant she had staggered the fawning waiter with a long litany of allergies: mushrooms, eggplant, olives, sweet peppers, and on and on. It had spoiled Shanks' appetite.

Shanks wondered what had made Ed look so much older; the murder or the marriage. "This isn't private," he told him.

"I've got nothing to hide. Jeez, what are you doing here? You didn't fly in just to see me, did you?"

Shanks explained the purpose of his trip to California, and his visit to the jail. Ed seemed unsurprised that his ex-wife had rushed to the rescue. "Jean's right, Shanks. I didn't kill Abitha. I'm nuts about her."

"Let's see if the newspapers had the story straight. They said you were at your beach house in Malibu, alone, working on a book."

"Bingo."

"Don't you have an office in your home?"

"Naturally. I do most of the writing there, but this was different. I was trying to outline a new novel. I had about two hundred index cards covered with characters and plot points. I wanted to spread 'em out on the floor and mix them around for a few days until I figured out the structure. I need a big room for that, bigger than my office, and Abitha – well."

"She didn't like it if you made a mess of the living room."

Ed looked sheepish. "Pretty much."

"Were you expecting her to drop by?"

"No. She was supposed to be on location overnight, staying in a hotel by the Nevada border. Apparently filming ended early and she came home."

"Apparently. Did you talk to her that day?"

"No. I was still asleep when the limo came. The next time I saw her—" He took a breath. "Around nine the next morning. I went out to the carport and there she was."

Shanks nodded. According to the newspaper articles Abitha had been found dead; her head bashed in by a bottle of champagne from the picnic basket which the police had found next to her. If footprints or fingerprints had been found the press didn't know about it.

"I take it you didn't hear anything odd during the night?"

"You know how loud the ocean can be. And besides, when you're in the middle of plotting a story, jeez…"

Shanks understood. He had burned out many a tea kettle in the throes of creation; ignoring the desperate whistle as he wrestled with a stubborn character or a sticky plot point.

"The papers say Abitha left your house around eight P.M. Presumably she picked up the picnic basket – it was prepared by Brass Lion Catering – and headed over to your beach house. How far away is that?"

"That time of night, just under an hour." Ed fidgeted. "What do the cops think? My wife surprises me with a picnic dinner, so I meet her in the carport and kill her? Crazy."

Shanks shook his head. "Not at all. I can think of a dozen ways it could have happened, so I'm sure they could too. You could have had a visitor there when she arrived." A lover, he didn't say. "Or you two could have had an argument."

"We never fought!"

"Oh, come on, Ed. The papers said you were separated last year."

"She was in Argentina filming a movie. I was here working on a book. *That* was the only separation. Jeez, Shanks, you know the press. If they can't find dirt they make it up. Otherwise nobody buys their fishwrappers."

"And you were in couples therapy."

"This is L.A. If you aren't in *some* kind of therapy people think you can't afford it."

"So the only reason you were spending the night apart—"

"Was because she was supposed to be on location."

"Did she know you were going to be at the beach house?"

"Good question. I called around noon because I left my cell phone at home. I wanted her to know where I was in case she wanted to call me. She was on the set so I spoke to one of her assistants – Cheryl or Nina. I can never tell them apart. You'll have to ask them if they told her. What are you thinking?"

Shanks looked at the mirrored wall. "If she didn't know you were going to be there, maybe the picnic was for someone else."

Ed blanched. "You mean she was cheating on me. And her lover killed her."

"It's possible." Shanks could picture Abitha arriving at the beach house with another man, discovering her husband's car in the carport. Lust turns to guilt and anger. The disappointed lover picks up the champagne bottle—

Oh yes, he could write that scene quite convincingly.

"That's nuts, Shanks. I don't believe she was cheating on me. I just don't buy it."

"Well, let's put it aside for now. Detective Cranepool showed me a list of the contents of the picnic basket. Let's look it over. Maybe something will leap out." For example, if there was food Ed didn't like it might support the lover theory, but Shanks didn't say that.

"Let's see. There was a roast chicken. Two champagne glasses." Shanks tactfully ignored the bottle itself. "A loaf of French bread. Some spreads: caviar, tapenade, salsa. An assortment of crudités."

"Of what?"

"Sliced vegetables, suitable for dipping. Tarts for dessert. Sounds like a nice meal. Anything there you wouldn't eat?"

"You know me, Shanks. I'll eat almost anything. Jeez, I'm not picky."

That was true. He was just the opposite of Abitha, who had been fussy, hyperallergic, nearly anorexic—

Shanks frowned. 'There's something wrong with that list." His eyes ran down it again. "Tapenade. Why would she buy tapenade?"

"I don't know. What the hell is it?"

"A dip. Or a spread. The main ingredient is olives. Wasn't Abitha allergic to olives?"

Ed's eyes rolled up and Shanks knew he was mentally tracing that long list of allergies. "Yeah. Olives were definitely a no-no. You sure this taffy-odd has them?"

"Tapenade. Definitely. So why would she have ordered a food she was allergic to?"

"*I* like olives. Maybe she ordered it for me."

Shanks didn't think a woman as self-absorbed as Abitha would ever deliberately buy a food that could make her sick, not if it had been Ed's favorite dish on earth. He couldn't think of a polite way to say that, though. "Maybe. But what if she didn't order it at all?"

Ed's eyes widened. "Shanks, you amaze me."

"Mr. Longshanks, you disappoint me." Cranepool shook his head mournfully. "When I said you could speak to Mr. Godwen I didn't expect you to play *detective*. We do this for a living, you know."

So here came the dressing down. Shanks had walked into the police station expecting it, but now that it had finally arrived he found himself getting irritated. "Look, just find out who bought the picnic and I'll get out of your hair."

The detective sighed and folded his arms. "In spite of what you might read in *cheap fiction* the police are pretty competent, Mr. Longshanks. We checked that this morning."

"So who bought the picnic?"

Cranepool grinned. "Abitha Peel."

Damn. Shanks forced himself not to shrink under that smug smile. "Is that right? I can't imagine why she chose tapenade. Was the picnic basket a pre-packaged thing?"

"Nope. She chose everything from the caterer's website and had her assistant call it in."

"She didn't do it herself?"

"Movie stars don't do *anything* themselves, Mr. Longshanks. The assistant also picked it up for her. The caterers say he got there ten minutes before closing time."

"Really." Now it was Shanks' turn to smile. "That's very interesting."

"Why is that?"

"Because Ed told me his wife's assistants are named Cheryl and Nina. Which one do you think is a *he?*"

Cranepool called in a cop named Ramirez and together they gave Shanks a master class in phonemanship. Within an hour their calls established any number of things.

For example: Abitha Peel had no male assistants. The offices of her agent, publicist and lawyers (*my*, thought Shanks, *what a lot of people it takes to maintain a movie star*) all had male employees, but none of them admitted to calling the caterer and there was no obvious reason to think one of them was a liar.

As for the caterers, they only remembered their disappointment that the star hadn't come in person to pick up the food. They could say nothing about the man who did except that he paid cash.

"You realize who the prime suspect is?" Cranepool asked.

Shanks frowned. "No."

"Your buddy, the husband. *He* could have bought the stuff to surprise her."

Shanks thought about it and then shook his head. "Not a chance, Detective. I can imagine Ed killing his wife in a fit of anger, but there is no conceivable passion that would make him order a catered picnic."

Cranepool scratched his chin. "Not a great romantic, huh?"

"A six-pack and a bucket of chicken would be more his idea of a big gesture."

The cop sighed. "We'll have to go talk to the caterers again. See if they can stretch their memories."

"I wonder. This was an upscale place, right? Champagne, caviar, and so on?"

"Right. So?"

Shanks raised an eyebrow. "Security camera?"

By the time the security video arrived Shanks had called Cora at the hotel to say he would be late. "The meeting with the network went pretty well," she told him. "Their latest offer wasn't hilarious; merely amusing. Pat thinks that by tomorrow they may be up to serious money."

"That's great, dear."

"How's Ed holding up? Do they really think he did it?"

At the other end of the squad room Detective Cranepool had popped the tape into a VCR and was frowning at the grainy picture.

Shanks smiled. "I think they're coming to their senses. I'll be home as soon as I can."

He hung up and hurried over to the video machine. 'That's not Ed Godwen."

"It sure isn't," said Cranepool. He sounded like that was a personal insult. "So who the hell is it?"

The man who claimed to be Abitha's assistant was a thin, sharp-nosed fellow in his thirties. He possessed a smile that Shanks would have crossed the street to avoid.

"What the hell is he smirking about?" muttered the cop.

It was almost time for the shift change and patrolmen passed by on their way to roll call. One of them stopped and stared at the screen. "Huh. When did *he* get out?"

Shanks and Cranepool turned to look at the patrolwoman. Her name tag said *Kesney.*

"You know this guy, Gloria?" Cranepool asked.

"Sure. When I was a rookie I helped escorted him to the courthouse once." She frowned. "What was his name? Logan? No, Slocum. A real bugcase. He'd been stalking one of the newscasters; thought they had a big romance going. He used to call up restaurants and make reservations in her name. Then he'd go and sit at the table and get mad when she didn't show up. Of course, it was all in his head. She didn't know he existed."

"Hell, yes," said Cranepool. "It's coming back now. Didn't he finally kidnap her?"

Kesney nodded. "Grabbed her outside her house and took her at gunpoint to a restaurant where he'd booked a table. Of course, it didn't take the maître d' long to realize this was something worse than a lover's quarrel and he called 911. Everything ended peacefully and Slocum went to jail."

"Looks like he's out now," said Cranepool.

"Yeah. Is he still making reservations at restaurants?"

The detective generously let his guest handle that one. Shanks shrugged. "I guess he thought Abitha Peel was more the *al fresco* type."

"So, apparently this Slocum had been stalking Abitha for a while," Shanks told Cora, back at the hotel. "He was convinced they were going on a picnic together, just like he had been convinced the newscaster was going to meet him at a restaurant."

"Creepy."

"Extremely creepy. He ordered the food in her name and picked it up at the caterer. Then he went to her house and followed her when she left. When she headed toward the beach it fit right into his fantasy."

"So when they reached the beach house," said Cora, "he took out the picnic basket and went to greet her—"

"And Abitha had no idea who he was. Probably screamed her head off. Slocum lost his temper and hit her with the champagne bottle. The cops are looking for him now."

"Well, thank heavens the police figured it out," said Cora.

"Absolutely." Shanks had downplayed his role in the story. Otherwise Cora would have regaled the guests at every party for the next five years with the hilarious tale of hubby playing detective.

"By the way, what was the favor the officer wanted?"

"Oh that." Shanks grinned. "Cranepool wants me to introduce him to Mitzi Torricelli."

"And who in the world is she?"

"An actress. She played the female lead in that awful film they made from my second book. You remember, she was the redhead with the un-realistically large—"

"I remember. Did you help him out?"

"I promised to call the producer. That guy owes me a favor, anyway, considering I didn't sue him over his guerilla accounting methods."

"So Ed is a free man again?"

"Yup. Staying at a hotel, while he decides what to do next."

Cora nodded thoughtfully. "The question is whether she'll take him back."

Shanks stared at her. "Who'll take who?"

His wife gave him the look that said he was being remarkably dim. "Whether Jean will let Ed come back to her, of course."

"What makes you think he'd want to? *He* divorced *her*, remember."

Cora shook her head. "Oh, he'll *want* to. Some men can't bear not being married." She had the good manners not to look at him when she said it.

"Well, if he *does* want to come back I'm sure she'll take him. I mean, look at all the trouble she went to to get me to, uh, visit him in jail. Surely that shows she still cares."

"Not necessarily. It might have just been closure. She passed the buck to you and wiped her hands." Cora smiled. "Jean is quite a lady. I don't blame you for having a thing for her back then."

Shanks frowned. "Did I tell you about that?"

"Of course. The day you introduced me to them you told me Ed had stolen her away from you."

It was typical that she had remembered that, he thought, and even more typical that he had not.

Cora was staring into the distance. Shanks knew the look well; the thousand-mile gaze of a writer in the throes of creation. "You know, I think I could get a novel out of this."

"No fair!" he protested. "I saw it first."

"Relax. What are you thinking of?"

"A stalker turned serial killer who reproduces classic movie scenes in his crimes. What about you?"

"A woman whose ex-husband becomes a widower. She has to decide whether to take him back. I'm not exactly trodding on your toes."

"No, you're not." He shook his head. "Amazing, isn't it? How can two writers hear the same facts and draw completely different inspirations?"

Cora stood up. "Well, you wouldn't want us to be *too* much alike, would you, Shanks?"

"I suppose not. Where are you going?"

"To take a bath. Why don't you call room service and order some dinner? Wine, too."

"Great idea." Shanks picked up the phone with a grin. He was thinking, not for the first time, that mysteries made better reading but in real life romance was a lot more fun.

This story made it into HITCHCOCK'S, April 2005, thereby establishing Shanks as at least a two-trick pony. I don't know what gave me the idea, but I dislike southern California, and I loathe olives.

One of the things I like best about the story is (brace yourself for a bit of literary fancy-pantsism) the unity of theme here. With the possible exception of Ed and Cora, everyone in the story is motivated by romantic impulses. Even the crazed killer.

And I also like the fact that the middle-aged writer couple clearly have an active love life. Good for them.

SHANKS GETS MUGGED

Someone was shining a bright light in Leopold Longshanks' eyes and asking him foolish questions.

"Who's the president, sir?"

"Millard Fillmore."

The paramedic lowered his flashlight, the better to stare at him. "Who?"

Shanks sighed. A dark street in downtown Madison was no place for a quiz on American history. "Look, I know the president, and what city we're in, and even the day of the week. I lost my wallet; not my wits."

"This is just standard procedure, Mr. Longshanks. When we find a man lying in the gutter—"

"He knocked me down, that's all. I would have stood up as soon as I caught my breath."

"—especially a man of your age—"

Shanks made a face, which made his head hurt more. "What does my *age* have to do with it? A man turns fifty and suddenly it's as if he's from an alien species. I start getting these magazines I never subscribed to, and offers to take discounts, like I'm a charity case—"

"Sir? Are you sure we can't give you a ride to the hospital?"

"Just give me a lift home. And *you*—" He said to the policeman who stood nearby, looking bored. "Remember that description I gave you. Especially the sneakers. White high tops with two wolves on the side—"

"Dos Lobos," said the cop. "Very popular among gang members this year. Must be a thousand pairs in this county alone."

"But how many of them have green and red paint spatters all over them? My God, did you even write that *down*?"

And then Cora's car came speeding up. She had been dragged away from her bridge game by a terrifying phone call from the paramedics. He was sure to hear about *that* later. "Shanks, are you all right? They said your head was bashed in!"

"Slight exaggeration, my dear. The mugger knocked me down and I banged my head. I'm fine now."

"He really should go to the hospital," the paramedic told her.

"He won't," Cora assured him.

"Damned right," said Shanks.

"Hospitals terrify him."

"Now wait a minute!"

"I'm taking you home right now," she said, putting a hand on his shoulder. "What were you doing downtown at this hour anyway?"

"Going for a walk to plot out a book. Which used to be safe in this town, even after dark."

"These aren't the good old days, darling. You should know better. A man of your age…"

"I wish people would stop saying that. At my age a writer is just reaching his creative *peak*."

"Get in the car, Shanks. We have to go home and start making phone calls."

"Phone calls?" He stared at her. "I get mugged and you want to alert the media?"

Cora shook her head irritably as she climbed into the driver's seat. "He took your wallet, right? That means we have to cancel our credit cards, and probably half a dozen other things they can figure out from the dozens of receipts and checks you usually carry around in that thing."

She was right, of course. Which gave him something else to be mad about.

Shanks spent the entire next day wrestling with the paperwork that accompanied a mugging. Talk about adding insult to injury. Going to DMV for a new driver's license was just one of the pleasures.

Then Cora made him go to his doctor, "just to make sure."

Dr. Krebs was unimpressed by the lump on his head. "It's the lump in your gut you ought to be worrying about, Shanks. You need to exercise and lose some weight. A man of your age…"

By the day after that things had returned to relatively normal and Shanks could get back to work. The only problem with that plan was that his latest novel idea had curled up and died in his hands. Worse, this was the third time in a row that had happened. And this left him with nothing to do but sit in his home office and brood.

He called the cops, mostly to confirm what he already knew: investigating a mugging without injury was so low on their to-do list that nothing short of the perpetrator strolling into the police station with a signed confession was likely to get their attention.

And then, back to brooding. It wasn't the money, damn it. It wasn't even the inconvenience of replacing credit cards and so on. It was the *principle.*

The kid had pointed a knife at him and demanded his wallet. No, let's be honest. He had said: "Give me your wallet, old man." And that stung too.

Shanks scowled at the computer screen where his next novel didn't seem to be developing.

All right, he thought. *If you can't write just now, what else can you do?*

"You know," he told Cora at dinner that night, "I've been thinking and I decided you're right."

She stared at him. "Well, let me get a pencil."

"What for?"

"I want to mark this day on the calendar. Celebrate it every year."

"Very funny."

"So, what exactly am I right about?"

"You were complaining that there isn't room in this house for two novelists. We keep bumping into each other, interrupting when we're on the phone, and so on."

Cora frowned. "I vaguely remember saying something like that a few months ago, back when you were thinking of writing a novel about an opera singer and insisted on blasting the stereo at full-volume for inspiration. And *now* you decide I was right?"

"Your wisdom takes time to absorb."

"No doubt. So, who's moving out?'

"I thought I'd try renting a little office, maybe over in Morristown. Just for a few months, to give it a try. What do you say?"

His wife looked thoughtful. "Why not?"

"Really?" He had expected more resistance.

"Sure." She smiled sweetly. "The change might be good for you."

Ah. Cora thought he was trying a new way to break out of his writing slump. Well, fine. That was a lot easier than explaining what he really had in mind.

Back when Shanks was younger and foolish enough to take advice from a brother-in-law, Cora's brother Bob had convinced him to set himself up as a business. This was supposed to have tax advantages once Hollywood started buying Shank's books and pouring down a flood of money. Hollywood cash continued to be somewhere between a drought and a light mist, but he still had the paperwork for a company name.

He used that name to sign up for a small second floor office in Morristown, a few miles from home. The landlord supplied a desk and a couple of chairs, so all that he needed to bring from home was his computer and a file cabinet.

Then came the important part: decorating. Before Cora morphed into a novelist she had run an art gallery for a while and she still had an extra room full of paintings she had purchased from starving artists – most of whom deserved starvation in Shanks' opinion. With her permission he took some of the more bizarre paintings to his new office. Then he picked up some art magazines at the newsstand.

And finally he wrote an ad to go in the local newspaper:

FIVE HUNDRED DOLLAR REWARD
To the owner of a pair of
White High top Dos Lobos Sneakers
Spattered with paint
Seen in Morris County on April 3.

April third had been the day before the mugging. The ad ended with his company name and the office phone number.

The ad appeared on Sunday. On Monday the phone calls started. As Shanks expected he received calls from a number of people who would be happy to paint their sneakers any color he wanted in return for five large, and most of them were quite irritated that that didn't feed the bulldog.

One pilgrim seemed determined to call back with every possible combination of colors until he hit on the winner so Shanks had to pull out his back-up ploy. "Where in Morris County would those sneakers have been seen on April third?"

Uh. The caller had no idea what the right answer was.

Shanks didn't know either; it was a bluff. But it successfully chased off a few phonies.

On Tuesday morning a woman called. Her voice was young and hesitant. She said her name was Brook. "Why do you want to know about those sneakers?"

This was promising. If he had been writing the scene, that was just the sort of dialog he would have created. "It's for an art project," he explained. "But let's make sure we're discussing the right sneakers. What color is the paint?"

"Red and green. What sort of art project?"

"It's too complicated to explain on the phone. Why don't you bring them in and we'll discuss it?"

"They're not *mine*. Don't you know whether it was a man or woman who was wearing them?"

"Sorry. I assumed you were calling for boyfriend, or a relative. He can come in too."

Shanks had considered the possibility that the mugger might recognize him, but he concluded it was unlikely. On the mean streets of Madison he had been wearing a raincoat and a soft hat, and the mugger had only seen him for a few seconds under a streetlight. Granted, the bad guy could have spent many happy hours memorizing the picture on Shanks' drivers' license, but why would he bother? Shanks had

decided to introduce himself as Mr. Lipton, the name of the previous office tenant, which was still visible on the door.

On the other hand, Shanks was pretty sure he would recognize the
mugger. And the man who came in with the girl named Brook was definitely not him. Paul, as he introduced himself, was the right age, early
twenties, but too thin and short, and his greasy hair was too long and
light.

He was wearing Dos Lobos sneakers, but they were black high-tops,
with nary a paint drip in sight.

It was hard for Shanks to guess Brook's age. She might have been
eighteen but she had added a few years to her appearance by make-up
and perhaps through hard living.

"You serious about the five hundred bucks?" Paul asked

"For the right pair of sneakers. Have a seat. Can I get you a coffee?
Tea?"

Paul shook his head. Brook, sounding rather surprised with herself,
asked for a tea.

"You see," said Shanks. "I'm an agent for a number of artists." He
gestured at the strange spangled and shiny canvases on the walls. "I put
that ad in at the request of a client of mine who wants to remain anonymous for now. He is an artist, a really talented fellow who works mostly
with conceptual and performance art. Are you familiar with the *genre?*"

His guests shook their heads. Paul was frowning; Brook was
wide-eyed.

"Well, you can read about it some of these magazines." He pointed
to a few issues he had spread open on the table. They featured articles
about one budding genius who shaved his head and sold the bag full of
hair for ten thousand dollars, and another who simply stood in front of
an empty gallery and shouted obscenities at people who came to see the
art.

Shanks figured that compared to those alleged Rembrandts the project he was about to describe would seem like Norman Rockwell.

"This is *art?*" asked Paul, showing better taste than Shanks would
have given him credit for.

He laughed. "The people who pay for it seem to think so. Now, it happens that my client fell in love on April third, and he decided to make an art project out of everything related to that experience. He has kept the clothes he was wearing, and that his new sweetheart was wearing, and the menu from the restaurant—"

"And that's *art?*" Paul repeated.

"I think it's sweet," said Brook.

Shanks smiled at her approvingly. "Well, it happens that one of the first things my client and his new love chatted about was a pair of sneakers they had both noticed. So, naturally he wants to add them to the *assemblage.*"

"And he's going to *sell* this stuff?" said Paul skeptically.

Shanks gestured toward the magazines. "You'd be amazed at what people will buy if they think it's art. So, do you have the sneakers?"

"A friend of ours does," said Brook.

"Ah. Well, tell him to come in with them and if he can tell me where he was on April third and it matches what my client told me, he gets five hundred dollars."

"What about us?" asked Paul.

Shanks dropped his bushy eyebrows. "Hmm. A finder's fee would definitely be in order. Ten percent would be typical. So you get fifty dollars when I approve the purchase of the sneakers."

Paul wanted to dicker for more but Shanks suggested he should take it up with the owner of the sneakers. Why shouldn't the lucky man share with his friends?

The friends brought the lucky man with them later that day. He looked confused and belligerent. His name was Carl Nesmith and Shanks thought he might have been the mugger.

Then he spoke and Shanks *knew*. It wasn't easy to keep his poker face on. Nesmith was shorter than Shanks remembered – a knife in your hand adds several inches to your height, apparently – but it was him.

Shanks repeated the cover story he had told Nesmith's friends.

Nesmith seemed less curious than the others had been. Certainly he didn't show any interest in Shanks. "Here's the shoes," he said. "Where's the money?"

Shanks looked at the sneakers and repressed a shudder. He remembered lying in the gutter and staring at those big ugly shoes, expecting them to start kicking him.

"Where were you on April third?" he asked. He tried to keep his voice neutral, but he thought it sounded like the stereotype of a police interrogation: *Where were you at midnight on the night of so and so?*

Nesmith listed a few places, a liquor store, a park, a store. It seemed so mundane; shouldn't muggers spend their day in opium dens or gang headquarters, or something?

"Ah, Verona Park. That's where my client saw the sneakers. So we're definitely on the right track." Her beamed at Nesmith and his friends. "I'll write out the checks. Just fill out these forms."

"What forms?" asked Paul. "You didn't mention any forms."

"Just a receipt, and a standard release. You realize, this all becomes part of the provenance of the art work. It needs to be properly documented."

"Why isn't the *artist* doing all this work?" asked Paul

Excellent question, Shanks thought, silently cursing him for it.

"You know how it is with the creative types." He raised a bushy eyebrow. "They come up with an idea and then someone else has to do the hard part. But rest assured, he'll be there to take all the credit."

All three of them nodded, apparently familiar with *that* type of person.

"You really need my Social Security Number?" asked Nesmith.

"All part of the procedure." Shanks assured him, as he scribbled a signature on the checks. It could have read Longshanks, or Lipton, or Norman Rockwell.

It wasn't until the next day, as he closed up his office for good that Shanks realized how much trouble he had made for himself. He now knew the name, address, and even the Social Security Number of a man he was morally sure was a criminal. What was he supposed to do with the information?

He hadn't thought that through.

Should he wait in a dark alley and hit Nesmith with a lead pipe?

Hardly his style. Besides, a man of his age – Now *he* was saying it!

Of course, he could take it to the Madison cops. He didn't know enough law to be sure they would be willing to act on his information. And even if they could they might consider it too much trouble, but at least that would be *their* fault, not his.

Besides, he suddenly realized, if they *did* act he might end up in the news as a comic character, a mystery-writer-turned-vigilante. He liked publicity as much as the next novelist, but for his *novels,* damn it, not for something that would look like a cheap publicity stunt. "The Miss Marple of Madison." No, thank you.

Could he remain silent? If he did that, then every time he read about a mugging in Morris County he would have to wonder if someone had been robbed – or worse – by the man he could have sent to jail.

The fact was, he didn't feel any great commitment to sending Nesmith to jail. The legal system did not have a fine report card on the subject of reform. But he had to do something to decrease the chances that the clown pulled a knife on some other unsuspecting wanderer.

And by the time he had his computer unpacked at home he knew what to do. He drove over to Truth Town.

Truth Town was a store that specialized in stuff that made the average citizen frown and say "Is that *legal?*" The answer was usually yes, with reservations.

If you wanted to spy on a neighbor, surreptitiously record a phone call, or do a background check on your daughter's fiancé, Truth Town could sell you the gadgets and guidebooks. With each purchase of one of the more dodgy items Sam Siriano, the owner, always provided a photocopy of the relevant laws, so that his customers didn't accidentally stray over the line while pursuing their no-doubt blameless purposes.

Oddly enough, most of his customers were people with legitimate uses for the equipment. There were private detectives, and lawyers, and even police officers. And occasionally, there was a mystery writer.

"So, what can I do for you, Shanks?" Sam asked. He was a hefty man with curly black hair and a nose as big and pointy as a hatchet blade.

"Last year you showed me a machine that changes your voice. You still have that?"

"Nah. We've got much better models now. The new technology just leaps along, doesn't it? Take a look at this little angel." He patted a machine that looked smaller and fancier than the one Shanks remembered. "This new baby lets you sound like a dozen different people, male or female. You want any cameras? I've got ones you stick in your necktie, your shoe…"

"Not today, thanks. But I could use your latest book on finding personal data over the Internet."

"I've got some beauties on that. You researching a new book?"

Shanks raised an eyebrow. "What else could I want these things for?"

"Natch."

"So, how much could an unscrupulous man find out about an individual over the web?"

"Depends how much your character already knew."

"Let's pretend he knew the target's name, address, phone number, and Social Security Number."

Sam let out a low chuckle. It sounded like something wild sighting its prey.

A week later Carl Nesmith was awakened by a phone call from his credit card company. The caller's voice was typical clerical: bored, almost mechanical. "Mr. Nesmith, we've had to close your account. If we don't receive some payment this week…"

Nesmith sat up, rubbing his eyes. "What are you talking about, man? I only owe like, what, five hundred dollars on that card."

"Our records say otherwise, Mr. Nesmith. Frankly, we should have never let your last two transactions through. You're well past your credit limit—"

"Just wait a minute!" He stood up and stared around his cluttered apartment. "I haven't used the card in, what, a week."

"That can't be right, sir. You purchased a dinner for two at the Chateau Gris in Livingston last night—"

Nesmith was outraged. "No way! I've never been to that, Chateau place. Someone must have stolen my card." He found his wallet on the bathroom counter. The card was right next to his driver's license. *Damn.*

"Look, you've made some kind of mistake. What card number do you have?"

The clerk read it off.

Damn.

"Okay, someone's screwing with my account. That's my number, but it wasn't me."

The clerk sighed, like he'd heard all this before. "Do you have your latest bill, sir?"

Nesmith shuffled hopefully through the a few piles of papers and found nothing. He really had to get organized. "I'll get back to you."

He hung up the phone and dug through a stack of junk mail on the coffee table. No luck.

The phone rang again. This time it was *another* credit card company. "I don't even have an account with you!"

"I beg to differ, Mr. Nesmith," said the clerk, this time a really snotty woman. "I have your signature, right here, opening the account last month. And now the money is due."

"This is fraud!" he shouted. "You have to get the money back from those people."

She laughed. "Don't count on that, Mr. Nesmith. Most of these transactions are donations to charities. Have you ever tried to get money back from one of those? You're better off just paying the bills."

"With *what?*"

When that witch was off the phone Nesmith gave up looking for bills and started looking for beer. At least *that* was where it was supposed to be. Just as he popped the top the phone rang again.

It was the finance company, telling him his check had bounced and someone would be coming to repossess his car if he didn't get to their office by five o'clock. After that, he stopped answering the phone, but that didn't stop them from calling, the bastards.

And then his *cell phone* rang. Almost no one had that number. He hit the button and heard yet another stranger, this one a man.

"Mr. Nesmith? Please don't hang up. I have some good news for you."

"Yeah? And what's that?"

"The phone calls you have received today were not from the people they claimed to be."

Nesmith almost dropped his beer. "Are you serious? What the hell do you think you're doing?"

"Just giving you a little demonstration of what your future could be like. Probably *will* be like in the near future. Oh, I should begin by asking if you believe that we could do in real life what we just pretended to do? You must know by now that we have your Social Security number, your credit card information—"

"Yeah, yeah, I get it. You're some kind of computer hackers. Either that or you work for the Feds, right? So, what the hell do you want from me?"

"Very simple, really Mr. Nesmith. We want you to stop breaking the law."

His eyes widened. "Law? What law?"

"Most of them. Oh, we don't care much about whether you double park, or even if you pay your taxes. Stay away from violence and we'll be satisfied."

Nesmith finished his beer. He had a headache. "Who the hell are you?"

"I represent an organization interested in rehabilitation. We have compiled a very comprehensive list of your activities, Mr. Nesmith. I guarantee the police would find it interesting reading."

He'll bet they would. He was sweating now. "What is this? Blackmail?"

"You can call it that, if you wish. We prefer to say we are showing you the consequences of your choices. If you choose to break the law again… well, the next time you are arrested, the police get our complete file on you. And then you start getting the kind of phone calls you received this morning, except that they will be real. You may escape from the police, but not from your creditors."

"What's my other choice?"

The mysterious voice left him hanging for a moment. "There's a technical college right in the town where you live. Our foundation has opened an account for you. It should pay for one semester in just about any course you want to take. It is *not* refundable, by the way, so don't imagine you can get the money."

Nesmith's head was aching. "Are you saying those are my choices? Go to school or go to jail?"

"That's it, Mr. Nesmith. If you get good grades we'll pay part of your future tuition as well. So, what's it going to be?"

He wanted another drink desperately. He wanted to hang up on these idiots and pretend this morning had never happened. Paul was supposed to pick him up in an hour. They were going over to the apartment of a friend who had gotten his hands on some stolen cell phones and—

Nesmith winced. He imagined he could hear the creditors calling again. And the cops.

"That technical college," he said.

"Yes?"

"Do they have a course in auto mechanics?"

Shanks hung up the phone and turned off the voice synthesizer. He didn't think it likely that Nesmith would change his life and go straight, but he figured this trick was at least as likely to make it happen as sending him to court. In any case, he had made more effort than the cops had.

Shanks frowned at the voice synthesizer, now taking up a chunk of his desk. It was probably too late to return it to Truth Town and try to get his money back.

Money. How much had this little exercise cost him? The synthesizer, the rented office, the modest price of some technical classes for his mugger. It made the actual amount Nesmith stole from him look inconsequential.

Then there was a month of his time wasted on the project, time he should have spent writing. But that didn't seem like such a major loss these days, not after three novels in a row had dropped dead halfway through the first draft.

Shanks began to wonder if this whole elaborate vengeance scheme he had dreamed up had been nothing more than an elaborate way to avoid starting on another novel. A crazy way to dodge writer's block.

He shrugged. Whatever it had been it was over now. Thank heavens he didn't have to think about it anymore.

Cora walked in, frowning at a folded piece of paper. "Shanks, we just got the credit card bill. What in the world did you buy at Truth Town?"

"Uh." Any sort of evasion seemed like a bad idea, especially with the evidence sitting on the desk next to him. "A voice synthesizer, dear. See?"

She saw. She was unimpressed. "Another gadget? This is going to be a tight month, Shanks. Do you think you could play with the toys you already have for a while?"

"Absolutely." He was thanking his lucky stars that he had paid the technical school out of his private account – what Cora called his "mad money," because he usually spent it on gifts for her when she got mad.

"Hmm," she folded the bill and looked at the voice synthesizer. "Well, I hope it works out for you, Shanks."

He raised an eyebrow. "What do you mean?"

She pointed at the machine with the hand that held the bill. "Obviously you bought that gadget because it figures in some new book you're plotting. I know you've been going through a rough patch this year, darling. So I hope this idea turns out to be one of your best."

Shanks stared at her. A series of images flashed through his mind, like pages turning. *A man gets mugged. He joins a victim support group and convinces the other members to join him in an elaborate plot of revenge and reformation...*

His heart pounded. For the first time in months his fingers itched with eagerness to get on a computer keyboard. "You know what, Cora? I think this just *might* be one of my best."

The reviewers and readers agreed. *A Man Of Your Age* was his most successful book in years.

This story was inspired by a bicycle accident. One minute I was riding home, the next thing I knew I was in a dark tunnel, staring at a blurry light and someone was calling my name. I had the peculiar sensation of being dragged backwards away from the light...

Sounds like I'm ready to write a book about my near death experience, doesn't it? Alas, the tunnel was the inside of an ambulance, the light was the sunny afternoon outside, the voice was a paramedic telling the hospital who to expect, and the sense of being dragged backward was, of course, caused by the gurney I was strapped to being pushed deeper into the vehicle.

So, no bestselling spiritual memoir for me, but the concussion gave me the starting place for this tale.

In some ways it's my least favorite of the Shanks stories, because it is so different from the others. The other stories take place during lunch, a cab ride, at most a weekend. This one takes months. And there is the scene from Nesmith's viewpoint. I tried writing it from Shanks' side of the conversation, but it didn't work.

In spite of this, the story made it to HITCHCOCK'S (December 2005), and a lot of people loved the last paragraph. I admit, I do too.

SHANKS ON THE PROWL

When the doorbell rang Leopold Longshanks tried to convince himself it was just a bad dream. The third ring persuaded him the real world was indeed trying to get his attention.

He looked over at Cora, who remained blissfully unaware of the rudeness of two A.M. visitors. She hadn't stirred when he came home at midnight and she wasn't moving now.

Shanks put on a bathrobe and stumbled out of the bedroom, down the stairs and up to his front door. Peeking through the peephole he saw a female police officer in uniform. She was a youngster, under thirty, but she had already perfected the cop look: bored and alert at the same time.

He pulled the robe tighter and opened the door. "Mrff?" he said. It was two A.M., after all.

"Excuse me, sir," said the cop. "Could you come with me for a minute? Your car has been prowled."

His response was automatic. "Is that a transitive verb?"

She met him frown for frown. "Excuse me?"

"I don't think *prowl* is transitive. You can prowl, or you can be *on* the prowl, but you can't prowl a car. Just like you can't *smile* a car. Intransitive verbs don't take an object."

The cop sighed, or maybe she was just taking a deep breath. "Sir, your car has been broken into. Would you come with me?"

He would, but first he went back upstairs and threw on some clothes. Cora still didn't wake up, even when he accidentally slammed a drawer shut. Twice.

Shanks' house had a two car garage but only one car fit in because the other side was stuffed with exercise machines, boxes of old clothes, and all the other barnacles that couples accumulate if they aren't smart enough to move or get divorced every few years.

It happened to be his car that was in the driveway that night, because he had been out at the semi-monthly poker game, which Cora called his "boy's night out," with an emphasis on *boy's*. She thought a man in his fifties should be beyond such things. Ah well.

He accompanied the cop – Officer Dereske, she told him – to his Toyota, where everything looked perfectly normal.

Shanks looked at the officer. "Are you sure someone broke into the car?"

She nodded. "We caught them down at the end of the block, Mr. Longshanks. They—"

"Call me Shanks. Everyone does."

"The burglars had a jimmie. That's a device for slipping into car windows to unlock—"

"I know what it is." In answer to her curious expression he shrugged. "I'm a writer. I write mystery novels."

"Oh. Have I heard of you?"

The only appropriate answer to that classic question was "How the hell do I know?" and that didn't seem the right thing to say to a cop, even at two in the morning, so he shrugged again.

He opened the car door and looked around the interior. "My CD case is gone. It holds about a dozen CDs. All jazz, if you're trying to sort the loot."

Officer Dereske made a note. "Anything else?"

"Nothing obvious. Oh, I usually keeps some change here, for parking meters. Less than a buck."

"How about the trunk?"

There was nothing in it but a set of jumper cables, which is how he remembered it.

Shanks frowned, thinking about what the cop had said. "Hey, if you caught the burglars down the street, how do you know they visited my house?"

"After we caught them we brought in the police dogs."

Shanks stared at her. "To do what? You already *had* them."

"We had the dogs sniff the kids. Then they followed their trail up the hill and showed us each house where they had stopped."

Shanks was fascinated. That would never have occurred to him. Use the dogs to chase down a bad guy, sure. But start with the bad guy and trace their paths *backwards?* He had no idea that dogs could be thrown into reverse, so to speak.

How could he fit that fact into his latest book?

They started back toward his front door. Shanks was thinking about what he was supposed to be feeling now. He had done enough research on crime over the years to know that he was supposed to be full of anger and a sense of violation: these punks had invaded his personal space, and so on.

Actually, what he felt was fascination. Imagine calmly strolling down a street in the middle of the night, burgling cars. And then there were the trail-sniffing dogs. All of this was far too interesting to waste time getting angry over.

He supposed they wouldn't let him meet the burglars. Too bad. He'd love to interview them.

Officer Dereske was getting an urgent message over her radio. She frowned; then shrugged. "Would you spare us a few more minutes, Mr. Longshanks? My sergeant wants to talk to you."

Shanks and Cora lived at 80 Lenape Hill Lane, near the top of a long, hilly block. Officer Dereske explained that the bad guys, a couple of teenagers, had parked at the bottom of the hill, walked to the top, and started working their way down the west side of the street, Shanks' side.

"My partner and I were on patrol and caught them with one house left on the block."

There were several police cars down there now and a steady flow of people moving back and forth between the houses on this side. Most of them were residents, Shanks noted, accompanied by cops. He was glad he had changed out of his bathrobe.

What's going on?" he asked.

"I don't know," admitted Officer Dereske.

The center of the action was the last house on the block. The owners had turned on a flood light that lit up the driveway and a police Humvee was parked in the middle of it. Police were leading his neighbors to and away from that circle of light.

When Shanks arrived the man in charge was just finishing with Ben Canote, who lived at 86 Lenape Hill Lane. Shanks and Canote were neighbors, but not friends. They had had words, usually about Ben's habit of calling city hall if a neighbor let his grass get an inch too long or his music a decibel too loud. Shanks had no patience for bullies.

"Hi, Shanks." He was smirking exactly like a schoolboy who had just tattled on a classmate.

"Good evening, Ben. They get anything from you?"

"Me? Not with the alarm system on *my* car. How about you?"

"The crown jewels. It's bankruptcy court for me." He liked joking with Canote, because Canote never got it.

The man in charge introduced himself as Sergeant Rice. After a few details about where Shanks lived and what he had lost the sergeant looked thoughtful. "You're a writer, Mr. Longshanks?"

"That's right."

"A *crime* writer, I understand."

"Mostly crime fiction, that's right."

Rice nodded. "I wonder if you can tell me what this is." He walked to the pile of loot in the back of the police SUV and flipped back a cover, revealing a large chunk of shiny steel destruction.

"Wow," said Shanks.

"Can you identify it, sir?"

"It looks like a semi-automatic machine pistol. Gloss finish. Is it a PCK?"

Rice looked impressed. "PCK 440, that's right. You seem to know a lot about guns."

Shanks shrugged. "I have to know something about them in my line of work. There are people out there who read mystery novels only to catch mistakes in the descriptions of gun. If you get one word wrong they will email you for months."

"So, do you own one of these guns, sir?"

Shanks shook his head. "I don't own *any* guns. I don't need to own them to write about them. Is this one even legal?"

"No, sir. But the young men we arrested say they found it in the trunk of one of the cars in this neighborhood."

Shanks blinked. "On Lenape Hill Lane? Semiautomatic, illegal *guns?*"

The sergeant nodded.

"Which car?"

"That's the question. The dogs indicate that they stopped at at least eight houses. But the youngsters don't remember which one had the gun."

"It wasn't mine, if that's what you're thinking," said Shanks. "You think they are telling the truth?"

Sergeant Rice smiled, a little ironically. "I think they would be happy to cooperate if it means less trouble for them. In fact that's part of the problem. Each of the two named a different house, but neither seemed really sure. If it went to court..." He stopped, with a shake of his head.

Shanks understood. The two young men had essentially said *You tell us which car you think it was and we'll agree with you.* If the cops took them to a district attorney with that story, and the D.A. was honest, he wouldn't be able to put either one of them on the stand. But if the cops could independently confirm which house it was, they could make sure the report reflected reality.

"Do any of your neighbors own guns?" Rice asked.

Shanks thought hard. He gazed around at the dark houses, and the shadowy figures still pacing up and down the hill. *Suburbia,* he thought. *I've lived in this house for ten years, and half the people on the block I wouldn't recognize by face or name.*

"The Cabrizzis," he said at last. "I know they fish. I don't know if they hunt, as well."

"And where do they live?"

Shanks pointed across the street.

Rice shook his head. "The kids say, and the dogs agree, that they stayed on the west side of the block. *Your* side. Any suggestions about this side?"

He had none. As tempting as it might be to think of a reason to point them at Ben Canote, he drew a blank. "Where there's one gun there might be more. A search warrant—"

The sergeant shook his head. "For half a dozen houses, because one of them maybe had a gun? No judge is gonna do that. Hell, no judge *should.*"

He sighed and pulled out a card. "If you think of anything, give me a call, Mr. Longshanks."

He saw Dereske going down the hill as he walked up. "Have any of the houses been eliminated, Officer?"

She frowned. "You aren't going to play detective, are you, sir?"

"God forbid. Good night."

When he walked inside he found Cora standing in the hallway in her bathrobe. "Shanks, it's three in the morning. Aren't you a little too old to be out all night playing cards?"

"I was home hours ago, dear."

"Then what were you doing outside? And who was that other voice I heard?"

He sighed. "That was a police officer. My car was prowled."

His wife frowned. "Is that a transitive verb?"

She was a writer too, after all.

He told her the whole story over a late breakfast. "Machine guns? On Lenape Hill Lane?"

"Only one gun," he corrected. "And a machine gun is fully automatic. This was only semi-auto—"

"Don't nitpick, Shanks. You know what I'm saying. It's crazy. This neighborhood – well. It should be *my* territory, not yours."

He knew what she meant. Cora wrote romances, not mysteries.

"I'm afraid we can't rely on crime to stay in the mean streets of downtown anymore." He stood up. "I'm going for a little walk. Do you want to come?"

Cora shuddered. "Out in the combat zone? No, thank you. Wrestling with this book outline is dangerous enough."

So Shanks walked alone, up and down the block, looking at the cars and houses, thinking about the neighbors he knew and the ones he didn't know at all.

There's no point in pretending I know these people well enough to know who would own an illegal gun, much less who would leave it in the trunk of a car. But there are certain things I do know.

When he came back Cora was busy in her office. Shanks went to his own and called police headquarters. He asked to speak to Officer Dereske.

"I'm just going off duty," she said. "You should speak to Sergeant Rice. He's in charge of the case."

"I'll tell you and you can tell him. I think you'll find that the gun came from 64 Lenape Hill Lane."

There was a pause. "What have you been up to, Mr. Longshanks?"

"Just walked up the street. Last time I checked I don't need a badge for that."

Another sigh. "All right. Why do you think it was that house?"

"Process of elimination. The burglars started at the top of the block, which is 100 Lenape, right?"

"I think so."

"Well, they didn't find the gun at the first house."

"Why not?"

"Because it *was* the first house. That would be easy to remember."

The cop sounded thoughtful. "Okay. I guess that makes sense."

"And the next house is where the hippies live."

"The what?"

"Hippies. I don't know their names, but the husband wears a pony tail with his business suit. And they always have a peace sign in Christmas lights on their front door in December."

"And you think because they put up a peace sign they wouldn't own a gun?" The scorn in her voice was clear.

"No, I think the car in their driveway is a Volkswagen Beetle. An original from the seventies, not the remake."

"So?"

"So, the trunk is in the *front,* and the engine's in the back. The thieves would remember that, don't you think?"

There was a pause. "Go on."

"Next is Ben Canote's house. He always brags about his car alarm, among other things. I assume the thieves saw the flashing light and skipped the car. Otherwise the whole neighborhood would have heard it."

"That makes sense."

"Next is my house. I know the gun wasn't there, but I don't suppose that's very convincing for you."

"Probably not. But go ahead with the others."

"The Sprewells on the other side of my house have an SUV. Again, no trunk. Your burglars may have taken stuff out of the back, but they wouldn't call that a trunk."

"Good point. Keep going."

"Next is 64 Lenape Hill. That's got to be the house with the gun. As I recall, a woman lives there with son. He's about eleven, or twelve. I don't know which of them would own the gun."

"Okay, go on."

"The next house has a pick-up truck."

"No trunk."

"Exactly. And the next one was the last one before they got caught, right?"

"I think so."

"They'd remember if it was the last house, wouldn't they?"

There was silence for a moment. "That all *sounds* good. I don't know if it will hold up."

"Well, run it past Sergeant Rice. And leave me out of it, okay?"

"That means we will be concentrating our investigation on you and on—" Papers shuffled. "The Eickwerths. That's the name of the family at 64 Lenape Hill."

"Pry away," said Shanks. "I can take the heat."

He spent the rest of the morning rewriting a chapter of his latest book. He arranged that after one of the bad guys died Inspector Cadogan had the brilliant idea of having police dogs follow his trail back to the hide-out.

Art imitates life, because life doesn't sue for plagiarism.

After a couple of productive hours Shanks found himself struggling with a comma that might or might not belong in a line of dialog. He decided it was time to take a break.

Cora was on the phone, no doubt telling a friend about the submachine gun in the suburbs. Shanks went out to check the mail.

Glancing down the block Shanks spied three police cars. Sure enough, they were centered in front of 64 Lenape Hill Lane.

None of my business, Shanks thought, but he was already headed down the hill. He passed the scene of the crime, as he thought of it, and proceeded to the end of the block, just a resident out for a stroll in his neighborhood. On the way back up – and why did the hill feel steeper every year? – he spied a familiar woman coming out the front door.

"Officer Dereske, don't you ever go off duty?"

The woman looked at him, startled. "Special circumstances, Mr. Longshanks."

She looked over her shoulder, and led him farther away from the police cars. "I don't think you'll have to worry about us investigating you."

"The Eickwerths confessed?"

She nodded. "That twelve year old son you remembered is nineteen, by the way."

"Really?" Shanks' bushy eyebrows rose. "Time does fly."

"As soon as we put a little pressure on Ms. Eickwerth, let her know our investigation had eliminated most of the houses—" She didn't quite meet his eye. "Well, she caved. Her son owned the gun. She wouldn't let him bring it in the house."

"Which is why it was in the car. Did he explain why he had the damned thing in the first place?"

Dereske shrugged. "He claimed he wanted to start a business selling things over the Internet. He says he didn't know some of them were illegal."

"Some of them? What are we talking about?"

"You'll read about it in the paper, I guess. He had some things in the basement of his house that his mother didn't know about."

"Guns?"

"Guns, silencers, some other stuff." She smiled. "More things you don't want to know about in your neighborhood, I guess."

"Too true. Well, I'm glad you solved the crime. Nice meeting you." He turned towards home.

"Mr. – Um, Shanks."

He turned around. "Yes?"

Dereske was frowning. "I think I was rude to you. That line about your playing detective."

"Oh. You were just doing your job."

"Yes, I was. But why did you give the information to me, instead of to Sergeant Rice?"

Shanks scratched his chin… "Is it going to help your career?"

"It certainly won't hurt. But why me?" She sounded bewildered.

"Ah. That was by way of apology." Shanks shrugged. "I checked the dictionary. *Prowl* is sometimes a transitive verb. If you can prowl a dark alley, I suppose you can prowl a blue Toyota as well."

Cora was in the kitchen, cooking dinner. By the look of the ingredients it was vegetarian, and no doubt nutritious, but it smelled pretty good anyway.

"Anything interesting in the mail?" she asked.

"Only if you need more credit cards. There are police cars in front of that green house down the block. Apparently they owned that gun."

"The Eickwerths? How old is that boy now, seventeen?"

"Nineteen." Shanks sat down at the kitchen table. "Cora, we have to get to know our neighbors better."

"I agree." She continued to chop parsnips, or turnips. Whatever they were. "Look on the table."

Shanks looked. She had written up and printed out an invitation to a meeting to discuss holding a block party.

"Perfect. You're brilliant as well as beautiful."

"And a hell of a cook." She dropped garlic into a pan. "Is the date all right?"

She had planned the meeting for the day of his next poker party, which he would have to skip.

Shanks sighed. "It's fine, dear."

They didn't know their neighbors, but they knew each other pretty well.

The first scene is true-to-life, right up to the point before the cop asks Shanks to accompany her down the block. The only difference was that when the cop who woke me up told me my car had been prowled I didn't have the nerve to ask her whether "prowl" was a transitive verb. I certainly thought it.

Here's a little peek behind the writer's curtain: Why was this story called "Shanks On The Prowl" and not "Shanks Gets Prowled," which seems to fit better with the other titles? I made that choice very deliberately.

Office Dereske is a little disturbed throughout the story about Shanks' kind attention to her. She is afraid she is meeting, not for the first time, a middle-aged man with an unhealthy interest in younger women in uniform. Hence her brisk and brusque attitude.

This is all under the surface, of course, and I want the reader to be vaguely aware that something is going on, but not clear on the problem.

The phrase "on the prowl" has the connotation of being looking for love, or a casual approximation thereof, and so the title was intended to get the reader's brain looking in that direction.

Of course, Dereske was wrong. That sort of flirting would never occur to Shanks. His motive, as the ending makes clear, had to do with a guilty conscience over verbs.

By the way, the officer was named for my friend and fellow librarian, Jo Dereske, author of the wonderful Miss Zukas mystery novels.

This story appeared in HITCHCOCK'S, May 2006.

~ First Interlude ~

This is not technically a Shanks story so, if you are a purist, skip ahead. But Shanks DOES appear in it, so if you are a completist, you should read on.

From 2007 to 2011 I blogged every Wednesday at Criminal Brief, the brilliant invention of my friend James Lincoln Warren. I will talk about that fine institution again in a few pages. But one thing you discover when you commit to this sort of thing is that Wednesdays come along with shocking regularity. Sometimes it seems like there are three or four of them every week. And you quickly run out of easy topics to fill your space. So one week I filled mine with this.

MISERY LOVES STRANGE BEDFELLOWS

On the night the Derringer Awards were announced I found a familiar character sitting at my kitchen table. He is in his fifties, thinning on top, with bushy eyebrows and his body shape suggests that he is fonder of good food than exercise.

He looked at me with resignation. "Well, you lost."

"What do you mean, *me?*" I asked. "Didn't you lose too?"

Leopold Longshanks shook his head. "Fictional characters don't win prizes. Stories do, and authors. But the characters never win or lose. We're innocent bystanders, so to speak."

"I had better explain to the readers of the blog that you are a mystery writer who appears in some of my short stories, like 'Shanks on the Prowl,' which was a Derringer nominee."

He frowned. "If they don't know your work, why would they read this website?"

"Because James Lincoln Warren is a marketing genius, I guess."

He snorted. "Anyone who gets people to write for free is some kind of genius, I suppose. Still, the readers are getting what they pay for."

"Don't insult the readers. Where would you be without them?"

"Same place I am now. In a bunch of stories that don't win awards."

"You have to rub that in, do you?"

He raised a hand dramatically. "Sorry if the truth hurts. Of course, unlike you *I* won an Edgar Award."

"A strictly fictional Edgar," I pointed out. "The Mystery Writers of America didn't give it to you, I did. To establish your credentials as a mystery writer."

"But it clearly means that I'm a better writer than you."

"Maybe you should write your own stories."

"Very funny. I wish I could. I do have a suggestion, though. I think my stories would work better if you let me solve more serious crimes."

"Oh, come on. You and I are in agreement about amateur detectives who find dead bodies behind every rose bush."

"Well I agree we shouldn't make a habit of it, but one or two wouldn't hurt."

"Come on, Shanks. You live in the suburbs and spend most of the day writing. How are you going to find murders to solve?"

"That's your problem, isn't it?" He looked around the room, bushy eyebrows dropped in a scowl. "All this philosophy is hard work. Do you have any Scotch?"

"I'm afraid not. Our drinking habits aren't the same."

"Yes, I know. You aren't me. As Conan Doyle wrote 'The doll and its maker are never identical.'" He grinned. "You know what amuses me? When you started writing about me I was a decade older than you. But you caught up."

"You should thank me for not aging you. Shouldn't you be vanishing back to New Jersey around now?"

"That reminds me. How come you never mention our home state in the stories? All those coy hints, like Verona Park, and Lenape Hill."

"I admit I like to put in references intended to tell people from the Garden State that that's where you live. But I don't want to distract people who think living there means you must have a Mafiosi for a neighbor."

Shanks brightened. "If I did, *then* I'll bet I could solve a murder."

"Oh, give it up. Say hi to Cora for me."

"And greet your lovely wife for me." He stood up. "Oh. Finish that story about the stolen book. It's kind of funny."

"Just the kind of praise every writer yearns for."

"Besides," Shanks said. "I want to find out how I solve it."

SHANKS GETS KILLED

Leopold Longshanks hated the whole idea of mystery weekends. He wrote detective fiction for a living, and did so with some skill, if he said so himself. So what made mystery fans think they could create new detective stories and act them out, as if they were the real thing?

Shakespeare has a fan or two but they don't dress up as Macbeth and Falstaff and start reciting new soliloquies, do they? If they did, they were at least courteous enough not to invite the Bard himself to participate.

Nevertheless, Shanks was about to lose a weekend to just such a shindig. He had no choice in the matter, so all he could do was face it with good manners and good grace.

"This stinks and I hate it," he announced.

"Tough," said Cora. She was driving, having concluded that if he were at the wheel they might accidentally end up in the wrong county.

His wife was the reason he was doing it, of course. The mystery weekend was the bright idea of the charity dedicated to eliminating the disease that had killed Cora's brother. In her eyes they could do no wrong. If Dixie Traynor, the madwoman who organized these things, decided one year that the charity's celebrity guests should come to some event dressed as frogs, then Shanks would have to get used to green paint or file for divorce.

"I don't understand why I have to be the victim," Shanks said.

"Dixie was just being nice," said Cora. "She knows you don't enjoy these parlor games, so she arranged for you to get your part done quickly. Then you'll have the weekend to yourself."

"While everyone else is busy." Maybe he could get some work done.

"And besides, the people playing characters have to act, Shanks, and that's not your strong suit."

Before he could respond to that slander she pointed. "There's the place."

The sign said MOUNTAIN LORREL INNE. That was something else to get irritated about; people who thought it was cute to misspell words in business names. Probably had an Olde Tyme Kurio Shoppe too.

The inn, or inne, seemed to have started life as a farmhouse a hundred years ago. Apparently the farmers had done well and added rooms over time. Now it was a determinedly quaint resort for city-dwellers looking for a weekend free of traffic jams.

Cora led Shanks through the lobby – heavily infested with calico and doilies – to where a giant of a man stood behind the counter. He seemed startled to see them, as if it were astonishing that strangers would come up to the check-in desk and expect to check in.

He introduced himself as Walter Lorrel, which explained the spelling. Shanks wondered if Walter, who was built like a football player, thought of himself as Mountain Lorrel.

Mountains aren't usually nervous, though, and Walter was. "Leopold Longshanks and Cora Neal," he repeated, as he tapped on a keyboard. "Let's see. Are you staff or guests?"

Staff? For a flabbergasted moment Shanks thought he was going to be asked to sweep floors and make beds. Cora figured it out first. "We're among the celebrity performers. I'm guessing that would be staff. The people who are paying to attend would be the guests."

"Ah," said Walter Lorrel. "Yes, you're right. Ms. Traynor asked that we put you in the west wing together. She thought – uh, you might like to be kept apart from the *guest* guests."

Good thinking. The people who paid to come to this event would mostly be dedicated mystery fans, and God bless 'em every one, but they could be unnerving. Especially the ones who thought that knowing your books meant they knew *you*.

After Walter had given them their keys – big, old-fashioned things which he managed to drop twice – and pointed them *toward the east* wing before his internal compass straightened out – they found their room and started unpacking.

They were interrupted almost immediately by a knock on the door.

Dixie Traynor was a bright-eyed little bullet of a woman, with her short hair dyed bright blond. "Cora, Shanks! So wonderful of you two to come *through* for us." She had just a trace of the accent of Georgia where she was born.

"We wouldn't miss it for the world," said Cora.

Shanks smiled politely and let silence give consent.

Someone cleared his throat in that artificial *here-I-am* way and all three of them turned to see a young man who had followed Dixie in.

"Oh, everyone! You have to meet Chet Chaplin. He's the genius—" Her drawl made the word three syllables long. "—who made all this possible."

The genius was in his twenties, with curly black hair and a pitiful goatee. He wore narrow black plastic glasses with very thick lenses. "Pleased to meetcha."

Dixie began to fill Cora in on the details of the weekend, so Shanks turned to the newcomer. "How exactly did you make this possible?"

"Oh. I wrote the storyline for the weekend. *Death In The Dark.*"

"So you're a writer."

"Me? No. I'm a computer programmer. But my hobby is RPG."

Shanks' eyebrows rose. "Which is?"

"Role-playing games. I write 'em or play 'em all the time."

"I didn't know there were that many mystery weekends."

"Mystery? Nah. This is small stuff. Mostly we do fantasy. Dragon slayers, vampires, and so on." He frowned at Shanks. "It's a real pain writing plots for characters with no magical powers."

"It's tough living without them too," Shanks admitted. "So, have you read a lot of mysteries?"

"Me? No. Dixie had me read the storylines from a few other mystery weekends. She said that was plenty."

Shanks sighed.

After Dixie and her pet computer geek left they settled down to look at the descriptions of the characters they would be playing. Shanks' part was easy because, as promised, he kicked the bucket almost immediately. But Cora's profile filled many pages.

She frowned at it. "This is awful."

Shanks had been approximately one-half of a successful marriage for so long that the words "I told you so" didn't come near his lips, and barely brushed across his cerebellum. "Oh?" was all he said.

"My character is a romance writer—"

"Typecasting." Cora really did write those, although she preferred the term *women's fiction.*

"But her life is like the worst romance novel you ever read. No, more like a bad soap opera. Her high school sweetheart disappeared in a plane crash. Her first husband was killed by a hit-and-run driver who was never caught. She makes mysterious visits to a small town in Vermont every year – and I'm supposed to subtly mention that in conversations? How do you slip that in?"

"I'm sure you'll find a way."

She shook her head. "That boy Chet has no idea what he's doing. I should have let Dixie go ahead with her first plan."

"What was that?"

"Having *you* write it."

Shanks decided to be grateful for small blessings.

By late afternoon most of the celebrities – mystery writers and spouses – had arrived and were gathered in the parlor of the west wing for a pep talk from Dixie. Shanks and a few like-minded friends slipped out onto the balcony overlooking the apple trees that grew beyond the inn.

"How the hell did I get talked into this?" asked Ed Godwen. He wrote techno-thrillers, and made more money than all the others put together.

"Well," said his wife Jean, "I *think* you're here because Shanks saved your fanny when you were arrested for murder."

"Oh, jeez. That's right." He turned a baleful eye on his friend. "Well, now we're even."

"No question," Shanks said.

Ed lit a Cuban cigar. The inn forbade smoking, but he had unilaterally decided the balcony didn't count.

"And why are you here, Ross?" asked Jean.

Ross Perry – spy fiction – shrugged. "Cora. That woman is a force of nature."

"This is her charity," Shanks explained. "She can get quite pushy about it. If I were—"

"Shanks!" The lady in question was at the door, calling sharply. "Get in here, all of you. They're starting."

"Time to meet our public," said Jean.

The guests had arrived in large numbers, each paying for a room at the inn, and a sum on top for the charity. Shanks looked around the big library, trying to separate the fans from the fanatics, and the would-be writers from the game-players who would have been just as happy at one of Chet's vampire-slaying parties. Each of them was now clutching a big canvas bag decorated with the charity's logo and containing the paperwork for their part of the weekend.

Dixie stood up to welcome them. "I'm so glad y'all could be here. As you know, we're expecting a crime to be committed this weekend, and we're gonna need help from each of you to solve it. And the one who does so will win a beautiful prize. Show them, Chet."

At the far end of the room there was a table loaded with pamphlets from the sponsoring charity. Shanks had noted that they were neatly divided between medical information and pleas for money.

Chet stood behind that table. Now he dramatically lifted the lid off a silver salver, a gesture that had been repeated by thousands of butlers in thousands of bad movies. He lifted the contents, a small book with no slip cover and badly worn boards.

"Ladies and gentlemen," said Dixie, solemnly. "That is a first edition of Dashiell Hammett's masterpiece *The Maltese Falcon*."

There were appropriate *oohs* and *ahs*.

"This rare classic was donated by an anonymous patron of our organization." Dixie smiled. "Frankly, it's worth a bundle. And to win it, all you have to do is solve the crime."

She reminded everyone of the rules. The writers-actors would be in character during certain specified periods and the guests could ask them questions only then. At other times, interrogations were strictly forbidden.

At dinner the authors were under orders to spread out and be charming. Shanks sat at a round table with Cora and four of the civilians, as he found himself thinking of the paying customers.

Two of them had stumbled in at the last minute. "Our plane was late," the female member of the pair explained to Shanks. "And would you believe it? They lost our luggage."

Shanks couldn't believe the plane part. "You *flew* here? For a mystery weekend?" Most of the guests had only needed to drive the few hours from the city.

The woman – her name tag said RUTH WAHL – nodded. "It's my husband, Tom. He's a nut for these things. We go to half a dozen around the country every year."

"Really." Shanks was always fascinated by the thousands of little worlds that went on around him unnoticed. "Is there a circuit?"

"Exactly. You'll see the same people at a lot of them. Some of them –" She indicated her husband with a roll of her eyes. He was talking to Cora, and didn't notice. "Get *quite* competitive. You can expect him to try and squeeze information out of you, even when you aren't in character."

Shanks' character would soon be dead, but he wasn't supposed to mention that. "Isn't that against the rules?"

"Tom says a real detective wouldn't care about rules, and wouldn't take breaks."

"Oh, I think even Miss Marple had to nap, and to wash her antimacassars occasionally. I take it you're not as competitive as Tom?"

"Not about this nonsense. No offense," she added hastily.

"Oh, I'm with you on the nonsense part."

"I'm a photographer and I suppose I'm competitive about that. But art isn't about prizes, right?"

"You may be asking the wrong person," said a cheerful voice on Shanks' other side. He turned and found a smiling man in his thirties. He was wearing a three piece suit, which made him a tad overdressed for the occasion.

"Shanks here was nominated for a major mystery award last year and didn't win," said the smiling man. "So he may be a little sensitive on the subject of prizes for art."

And nice of you to bring it up, thought Shanks. The stranger's name tag read PHILIP FALL.

"It's an honor to be nominated." Shanks had said it often enough to keep a straight face. "Are you a competitor, Mr. Fall?"

"Call me Phil, Shanks. Yes, for a lark. The fact is, I'm a mystery writer, too."

Uh oh. "Is that a fact?"

"My first book came out last year." He tugged promotional post cards out of his jacket and handed them to Shanks and Ruth, who had to put down their silverware to cope with them.

"I don't recognize the publisher's name," said Shanks.

"Oh, I published it myself," said Phil Fall, still smiling. "I got tired of the way the big companies rip off authors like us."

Like me, thought Shanks. *You're still a wannabe.*

He tried to turn back to Ruth, but Phil Fall was determined to talk writer-to-writer, even though half of the pair wasn't interested. Shanks tried not to be a snob, really. He wanted to be polite to aspiring writers – if the next generation was going to insist on arriving, he might as well be able to say he discovered some of them – but there was something about Fall's easy confidence that he had already earned a place at the grown-ups' table that got right up Shanks' nose.

All through dessert and coffee he had to keep reminding himself that this was a charity event and Mr. Fall was a paying customer.

When Dixie stood up to announce the next phase he had never been so grateful to hear her voice. "It's time for the first act of our little mystery, friends," she declared. "Please follow Chet into the library."

This was Shanks' big scene. He sat down at a table at the far end of the room, and the celebrity authors lined up behind him, as per instructions.

Unfortunately at the other end of the room Chet had decided to dramatically lift the dish cover again to show off the *Maltese Falcon* to a few of the guests. What a ham.

Shanks called Dixie over. "Can you get your genius to stop distracting the marks?"

While she shooed Chet, Shanks reviewed the pages in front of him. He was the only one of the celebrities with a prepared script. This was because he had to set up the plot for the whole weekend.

The one thing he couldn't object to was the character he had been given: an evil, greedy, manipulative publisher. Shanks felt he could play the part convincingly because he had known several excellent role models, so to speak.

"Welcome everyone," he said solemnly, "to this weekend to celebrate Karnage Books, and its authors. I'm Ken Karnage, the publisher and your host. I want to introduce my fine and successful stable of authors, some of whom, I might say, are more successful than others."

The authors behind him sounded appropriately irritated by that remark.

Shanks went on to complain about a downturn in the publishing industry and explain that most of these fine authors had not lived up to sales expectations, and some might be let go. Chet had included heavy-handed hints that some might be kept on only if they were "reasonable" in their money requests, and there were suggestions that blackmail might be going on, although whether the publisher was the victim or victimizer (or both) was not clear.

Then Shanks had to introduce each author, or rather, the character that each real-life author was playing. He didn't bother to keep them straight in his head. After all, his character would be dead in a few minutes, so what difference did it make to him?

He did think about what secrets his real life friends and colleagues might have.

Take Fiona Makem over there, with her curly red hair, green eyes, heavy make-up and cable-knit sweater. She had a lovely little brogue and was determined to set a mystery in each of Ireland's thirty-two counties, starting with *Death In Donegal, Slaughter In Sligo, and Plugged In Cork.*

She certainly wouldn't want the world to know that she had been born in Scappoose, Oregon, and that her mother's maiden name was Wishinski.

Then there was Leslie Warth, the wispy and eccentric author of cozies set in the world of art and antiques. It probably wouldn't help his reputation with his audience if they found out he had served in the infantry in Viet Nam.

And there was spy novelist, Ross Perry, calmly sipping club soda. Few people knew about his struggle with booze, including two busts for DUI.

And Ed Godwen—well, the whole world had heard about his arrest for the murder of his second wife. His present wife, Jean, was a stock trader, and we all assume they have dirty little secrets, don't we?

As for Cora, she somehow managed to put up with being married to Shanks, which was mysterious enough. He figured she didn't need any other secrets.

Shanks finished his speech with ominous threats that at least one of these fine authors – the fictional ones – would soon find themselves without a publisher. The civilians applauded politely.

And then, right on cue, the lights went out. "Stay calm, everyone," Shanks announced. "I'm sure they'll have everything back to normal in just—"

Someone tapped him on the back. That was his cue to stop speaking and slump over. Ken Karnage had just been killed.

In the pursuit of good acting Dixie had insisted that only the person playing the murderer should know who he or she was. However a familiar scent left Shanks in no doubt over who, to coin a phrase, done it.

When the lights rekindled Shanks was sitting forward, with his head and shoulders on the table. He hoped he wouldn't have to maintain the position long. It was quite uncomfortable.

But effective. One of the female civilians let out a little shriek, ending with a giggle. Jean Godwen quickly stepped forward. She had been introduced as a police officer who had written a memoir for Karnage Books.

"Everyone please move into the dining room while I examine Mr. Karnage. Don't talk among yourselves."

A minute later she patted Shanks on the shoulder. "All clear, Mr. K."

"Thank heavens. I was getting a back ache."

"As a corpse you should be grateful you can feel anything. That was a nice death scene."

"Thanks. What's next?"

"Go back to your room and relax. The rest of us have a murder to solve."

"I wish you the best of luck with it."

When Cora came to bed several hours later he was contentedly reading a Paul Cain novel – he read dead authors for pleasure. Living authors were market research.

Cora threw her purse across the room. "Those people are *crazy.*"

Shanks needed all his will power not to gloat. "How so, my love?"

"They ask questions no cop would ever ask, much less an amateur detective. 'Are you having any affairs?' 'Did you kill your first husband?'"

"Well," he said, "it's all for a good cause."

She gave him a harsh look, as if she suspected a little gloating had slipped in there. Maybe it had.

"This is going to be a *long* weekend," she said, and grabbed her toothbrush as if it had tried to escape.

"You have to help. It's a disaster!"

Shanks looked up from his page. He had been sitting on the porch enjoying a beautiful sunny Saturday morning while everyone else was inside trying to solve his murder.

Now Dixie, her shadow Chet, and innkeeper Lorrel were looming over him like patients expecting a bad diagnosis. Mr. Lorrel, with his bulk, was particularly good at looming.

"What's the problem?"

"The prize! Someone stole the prize!"

Shanks frowned. "Is this a metaphor? I mean, is someone trying to win by cheating, or did the book actually disappear?"

Chet nodded, his Adam's apple bobbing like a boat in a stormy sea. "That's it. The book is gone."

"Where was it? Did you leave it on the table in the library?"

"Yes," said Dixie. "We locked that room for the night, to make sure the little demons couldn't go in and prowl for clues. Honest to God, Shanks, if cops were as obsessive as these people, we'd *all* be in jail for something."

Shanks' bushy eyebrows dropped in a scowl. "How sure are we that no one slipped into that room?"

Dixie and Chet turned to Mr. Lorrel, who swallowed nervously.

"There are only two keys to that room. Nobody used mine."

"And mine stayed in my pocket," said Chet.

Shanks made a face. "You realize, that means there was only one time the book could have been taken."

They stared at him. "No. When?"

"When I was being murdered. While the lights were out, I mean."

He watched Dixie and Chet rerun the scene in their heads.

"I think you're right, Shanks," said Dixie. "But how did anyone know there would be a chance to steal it?"

"The name of this thing is *Death in the Dark*. It wouldn't take Sherlock Holmes to guess that the lights might go out at some point in the evening."

"Of course," said Chet excitedly. "It would have to be one of the people who was standing near the table. They could have tucked it into the canvas goodie bags we gave them."

"That woman I was sitting next to at dinner," said Shanks. "She's a photographer, and she was snapping pictures."

"I believe you're right," said Dixie. "Chet, go ask her if she has any from last night. But don't tell her about our... little dilemma."

When Chet was gone Dixie turned to him. "Now, Shanks, you have to—"

"Stop, Dixie. Stop right there." He turned to their host. "Mr. Lorrel, we need a moment alone, okay?"

The big man's eyes grew wide. "This is a decent place."

For a moment Shanks thought Lorrel believed that he – Shanks – had been overcome with illicit passion for Dixie. He shuddered.

"Well, of course it is," said Dixie.

"We've never had any trouble here," said the big man. He blinked. "Well, once a honeymoon couple had a fight and she walked into town in her nightie. But never any *real* trouble."

"I don't think there's likely to be any fist fights over this, if that's what you mean," said Shanks.

Lorrel turned his mournful face to him. "I mean *police*. I don't want them thinking this is the kind of place they need to patrol around all the time."

"Don't worry," Dixie assured him. "We won't be calling the cops."

"Wait a minute," said Shanks. "Don't make promises you can't keep."

"Oh, I'll keep this one." She turned to Lorrel. "Shouldn't you be back at the desk?'

"Me? Oh, right. But remember: no cops."

When the big man was gone, Dixie barely had time to open her mouth.

"Hold it right there," said Shanks. He gave her his most ferocious look. "If you're pulling a stunt, then this moment, *right now,* is your last chance to say so."

Her eyes went wide. "What are you talking about?'

"Maybe you had a great idea to liven up the weekend with a second crime. Maybe you have some actor friend ready to come in and play cop, looking for the missing book. But understand, if that's the case you have to tell me *now.* Because if you make me spend the weekend hunting for the book while you have it stashed in your car or something, then I swear to God, Cora and I will never lift a finger for your organization again. Are we clear?"

"How could you imagine I would do such a horrible thing?" Her eyes focused on a distant point and got a dreamy look. "But gosh, it would have been a great idea, wouldn't it?"

Shanks sighed. "Okay, I believe you. You don't know where the book is. Call the cops."

That snapped her back to reality. "Are you *crazy?* These people are *donors.* I can't drop a dime on them."

"One of them is a thief," Shanks reminded her. "Besides, they're all mystery buffs. They should love a chance to watch the pros at work."

"Come on. You don't believe that."

"I said they *should.* I admit they probably won't. But what choice do you have?"

Dixie's eyes narrowed cunningly. "That's easy. I have one of the smartest detective writers in the western world sitting around with nothing to do."

Shanks argued, but mostly to establish that he was doing it under protest. He figured he didn't have much choice.

Chet arrived with Ruth Wahl in tow. "What's going on?" she asked. "And why do you need my camera?"

Shanks didn't think Ruth was the thief, but he wasn't so sure about her husband. So he lied. "An allegation has come up that one of the contestants may have cheated."

"No kidding. Which of these kindergarteners couldn't play nice? Not Tom, I hope."

Shanks shook his head. "Not him. Obviously I can't go into details, but the accusation was that someone was looking at some papers that Dixie hadn't distributed yet. We're hoping your photos can clear it up."

Ruth opened her camera, shaking her head all the while. "I wouldn't put it past any of them, including my beloved spouse. They *obsess,* you know?"

Shanks had met plenty of fans. "I know."

"Do you have a laptop? I can download the pictures and they'll be easier to see."

Chet had one, naturally, and soon they were harvesting Ruth's crop from the night before. Shanks firmly turned the screen away from the photographer.

"Anything useful?" she asked.

"Perhaps." Shanks pointed at one group picture. "Chet, do you know all their names? They might have been in the position to see what was happening."

In fact, the photo showed the people who had been standing behind the display table just before the lights went out.

"Got 'em," said Chet.

"So, what do you see, Shanks?" asked Dixie, uncharacteristically hesitant.

"Let me glance through the rest of the pictures. Ms. Wahl, I notice you didn't take any during the blackout."

"I was afraid I might give away the plot. What if my flash showed the murder taking place?"

"Good thinking," Shanks admitted. He continued through the file and then stopped and sat up straighter, with what he hoped was the right touch of drama.

"Take a look at this." He swiveled the laptop to show Dixie and Chet a picture of his friend Ed Godwen forgetting to cover a huge yawn. "I think that clears it up."

"It does?" Dixie asked doubtfully.

"Definitely. The charges of cheating are refuted."

"Which picture did that?" asked Ruth, fascinated.

"Sorry. Can't go into details." He handed back the camera. "Thanks so much for your cooperation."

As Dixie led Ruth out he and turned to Chet, "So, who were those five people behind the table? One of them has to be the thief."

Two were Tom Wahl, the photographer's husband, and Phil Fall. "The self-publisher," he muttered.

The other three Shanks had not yet met. "But I'll have to," he told Dixie, "if you want me to look into this."

"I can't let you interrogate them," said Dixie. "I'll lose my job."

"Then we follow the novelist's rule," he told her. "When in doubt, make something up."

Cora was surprised, and none too pleased, that Shanks would be busy during her free periods – when she was not being "interrogated by amateur fascists," as she now described it. But since he was doing a favor for Dixie she couldn't complain. Not much, anyway.

"What do you know about fundraising?" she asked.

"Zilch. But Dixie has surveyed her regulars so often she figures they might like to see a different face."

He didn't want to admit to playing amateur detective. Dixie had arranged for him to interview a "random" assortment of contestants. Now all he had to do was get them talking.

Which turned out to be easy with the first candidate. The problem with Mary Iseley was finding a chance to ask a question. She belonged to Fan Category 7, the Wide-Eyed Bubbler, a breed that often seemed so out of it Shanks wondered how they managed to find the bookstore or, more likely, the library.

"This is so *wonderful,*" she said as soon as she was seated in the small parlor. "I love meeting all these writers, don't you?"

"They're an interesting bunch," Shanks admitted. "How are you do-ing at solving my murder?"

"Oh, I'm awful at that sort of thing," she said cheerfully. "I'm just here for the fun of it."

"Too bad you won't have a chance at the prize," he said. "A first edi-tion of a Dashiell Hammett book is pretty special."

She frowned. "I'm afraid I don't know him. Is he here this weekend?"

Shanks' pen fell on the desk. "No. He's been dead, uh, about forty years."

"I prefer living authors. I like meeting them, you know?"

"Is this part of the contest?" Tom Wahl asked. He tugged at his shirt, which was so big it made him look like a famine victim.

Shanks blinked. It was the same question – or at least the same thought – he had asked Dixie. "Come again?"

"You're one of the actors in the show. So I wonder if this talk is sup-posed to give me clues."

"I'm afraid not. My part ended when my character died. I'm just in-terviewing people for the charity. To see what they liked and didn't like."

"Huh. So they can have a better mystery weekend next time?"

"Well, I don't know about that. Dixie usually comes up with a new idea every year. "

"Then there's no point in talking to me. I only came because it was a mystery weekend. That's what Ruth and I do for fun."

"I heard you flew in for the event."

"Yeah, and the airline lost our luggage. Look at this." He pointed to his shirt. "I had to borrow it from the manager guy. He's not my size."

"So I see."

"And poor Ruth had to borrow clothes from that Dixie lady."

That explained why the photographer had come down to breakfast in a pastel lime and lemon outfit that didn't seem her style at all.

"But have you been enjoying the weekend?" Shanks asked.

"Not much. It's better when they use real actors, not these writer guys. No offense, but you aren't very good at this."

Shanks was inclined to agree, since he was having trouble getting to the subject. "What did you think of the prize?"

Wahl frowned. "Oh, that book? I didn't even notice it. The real prize is beating these losers to the solution."

"Are there a lot of people who travel from mystery weekend to weekend?"

"A few. I'm the best."

This simple declaration lifted Shanks' eyebrows. "Is there a league? Some official standing?"

"Doesn't need to be. I've won three competitions this year. Nobody else has even taken two. And last year..."

Shanks didn't really want to hear about last year, but he couldn't get Wahl to go until he pointed out that the next session of the competition was coming up.

Warner Bollister was exactly the kind of person Dixie was terrified of offending. He was Shanks' age, early fifties, but better preserved, which Shanks figured was because of his old money connections. Either his blue blood came with good genes or he had spent a bundle on strategic surgeries to make it seem as though they had.

"You can tell Dixie I don't care much for this year's fundraiser," he announced.

"I'm sure she'll be sorry to hear that," Shanks said. "What's wrong with it?"

"Detective stories. They're so childish, don't you think?" He waved an elegant hand. "I'm sure you make a living at them and I can't argue with that, but they're nothing for an adult to spend his time on."

Shanks couldn't think of a reply that wouldn't get him in trouble with Dixie, so he just smiled. "What *is* worth your time, Mr. Bollister?"

"Horses." The millionaire leaned forward, eyes gleaming. "I've told Dixie we should hold one of these events at the track. But she's afraid all the money would go to bets instead of to her precious charity."

"I'll mention it to her. What do you think of the prize this time?" He figured that since the novel didn't neigh or chew oats it wouldn't interest the man, but Bollister surprised him.

"*Maltese Falcon.* Damn good movie, but I never read the book. Don't have time for fiction. But I have friends who invest a lot of money in first editions. Small, easy to store, and the value escalates." He looked at Shanks, as if he were seeing him for the first time. "How much are first editions of *your* books worth?"

"In the high two digits. Of course, they'll be worth more when I'm really dead."

"Hmm." Bollister looked him up and down, appraisingly.

"What did he say about me?" asked Red Garrette. His nickname implied that his hair had once been red, but what was left of it now was mostly gray. He was in his thirties, and would be bald by forty. A nervous, twitchy kind of guy.

Chet had had trouble convincing Garrette to come for an interview, and stood behind him now. Shanks hoped he wasn't thinking about holding the man by force.

"What did *who* say?" Shanks asked. "Mr. Bollister?"

Garrette dismissed the millionaire with a shake of his head. "Wahl. The cheater."

Now *that* was interesting. "Are you saying Mr. Wahl has been cheating this weekend?"

"I'm sure he has, because he always does. But I don't have any proof this time. Not yet."

"I take it you two have been at some of the same parties before."

"Parties!" Garrette's scorn was rich. "These are *contests,* Mr. Longshanks. Competitions, and may the best man win."

"So you're after the prize?"

"What, some old book? That's just how they keep score. The important thing is beating cheats like Tom Wahl."

"How does he cheat?"

"Ha. Last year we were at a mystery weekend in Boston. The characters were played by actors there, and I caught him talking to one of the actresses during a break. He was quizzing her about her character!" Garrette raised his hands, as if calling on heaven to witness the abomination he was describing.

"That was it?" Said Shanks.

"That's *plenty,* Mr. Longshanks. You aren't allowed to talk to the participants about the case when other contestants aren't around."

"Did he have an explanation?"

"He *claimed* he was trying to ask the actress out. But that's nonsense. He's married!"

Chet Chaplin seemed to be having a coughing fit.

"That might not stop everyone," Shanks informed Garrette. "But the point is, you think Mr. Wahl would cheat to get what he wanted."

"Absolutely. Someone should hire a detective and stop him!"

"Good idea."

"Shall I bring the last suspect?" asked Chet Chaplin.

"Guest. Not suspect. I suppose you have to." Shanks grimaced. He had saved Phil Fall for last, hoping that he could solve the puzzle without interviewing the self-publisher.

No such luck.

"How you doing, Shanks?" said the man himself, strolling in. "Hey, I've got a question about audiobook publishers—"

"Maybe we can save that," Shanks said. "As you know, Dixie asked me to talk to a few of the participants about what they liked and didn't like about the weekend—"

It turns out Phil Fall had plenty of thoughts on that subject. In particular he thought things could be improved by having younger, *fresher* authors in the cast. "I mean, you guys are wonderful, Shanks, but I hear grumbling that people see the same faces at all these events. You understand?"

"I do. Of course, if you were part of the cast, you wouldn't be able to try for that prize."

"You mean the Hammett book?" Fall's eyes widened. "I'll be honest, Shanks, I'd *love* to win that one. I owe Dash a lot, you know? He really influences my work. Have you read him?"

The door to the library flew open and Dixie ran in. She skidded to a stop and stared wide-eyed at the three men who goggled back at her. "Shanks!"

They all rose to their feet. "What is it, Dixie?"

She opened her mouth, looked at Phil Fall, and changed her mind. "Phil, would you excuse us? I need to talk to these gentlemen."

The tall man left after Shanks promised to discuss audio publishers.

As soon as the door closed Dixie began vibrating again, as if someone had wired her to an outlet. *"It's back!"*

Shanks frowned. "The book?"

"Yes! Mr. Lorrel found it on a shelf in the pantry."

"How in the world did it get there?" asked Chet.

"Someone put it there," said Shanks. "And not by accident. Does Lorrel know when he last looked at that shelf?"

"After lunch, I think. But Shanks, don't you see? We have the book back. You can stop investigating!"

He made a face. "You can't *do* that to me, Dixie. Make me handle your dirty work and then tell me I can't finish it. I don't want to spend the next year wondering whodunit."

"Did the interviews give you any clues?" asked Chet.

"Clues? Tons. A solution? No." Shanks lifted his bushy eyebrows. "The key is obviously the fact that the book was returned. What was accomplished by stealing it for a few hours, other than ruining my day?"

That night, after dinner – which for Shanks was dominated by a lengthy discussion with Phil Fall – most of the crowd gathered in the library to watch a couple of classic crime movies. Shanks and a few of the authors slipped to the west wing for a chat.

"These people are bloody vultures," moaned Fiona Makem.

"All those personal questions," said Leslie Warth, with a delicate shudder. "I keep thinking they're asking about me instead of the stupid character I'm supposed to be playing. I may wind up confessing to *something*."

"Remember rule number one," said Ed Godwen. "Any of life's hardships is easier to bear after a drink. Anyone want a beer?"

Shanks helped pass them out.

Ross Perry turned him down. "I'm on the wagon."

"Oh, good for you, Ross," said Cora.

He laughed. "Don't tell my fans. Spy writers are not supposed to be teetotalers."

"They aren't supposed to have their licenses suspended for DUI either," said Shanks. "Here's a tonic water. Have any of you guys heard the guests talking about the prize?"

"The Maltese Falcon?" asked Fiona. "I heard the woman with the camera trying to convince her husband that it was *not* written by Humphrey Bogart."

"You're awfully broody," Cora said as they were getting ready for bed. "Dixie's surveys didn't go too well?"

"Well, she's satisfied with the results. It wasn't my idea of a fun Saturday. How about you?"

"Don't ask. Between trying to remember those awful clues Chet came up with, and dealing with the interrogations…" She shook her head. "If Dixie ever suggests doing this again, you have my permission to break her leg."

"With pleasure. Now we just have to decide on the right or the left."

"Both. And the worst of the interrogators is that insufferable Phil Fall."

"He is hard to take."

Cora fluffed her pillow, a little harder than necessary. "At least he didn't want to ask me about your murder. He was grilling me about finding a west coast agent to sell his book to the movies."

"The man has ambition," said Shanks. "I know the publishing world is changing, but self-publishing still comes with so much baggage—"

"Shanks? What is it? You've got that wild stare, like you just solved a big plot problem."

"Something like that," he said and turned out the light.

"I don't get it," said Chet. It was just after breakfast on Sunday and the various participants were still struggling with the tragic death of publisher Ken Karnage. "Dixie says there's no reason to keep asking questions, since we have the book back."

"For Pete's sake," said Shanks. "Can you turn off your curiosity like that? The desire to know what happened is in our genes. Not to mention the fact that it pays my mortgage."

"But Dixie—"

"Don't worry about her. You just get the right person in here when the session breaks up. Then you can leave or stay as you want."

He stayed, which restored Shanks' faith in human nature. "Have a seat."

Red Garrette sat down, frowning. "I already told you how I felt about this weekend. If you're looking for a donation—"

"Oh, you'll make a nice one," Shanks assured him. "Equal to the value of the book, I think."

"Why in the—" Garrette blinked. "What are you talking about?"

Shanks shook his head. "See, Chet? Simple questions, but unexpected ones. *That's* how to write a mystery."

Garrette looked at Chet. "Do *you* know what he's talking about?"

"You stole the prize, Red."

Garrette frowned. "What prize?"

"Dumb answer. Obviously I mean the prize for this weekend. You should have said: 'What? Is the prize missing?' or something like that. I hope you're taking notes, Chet."

Garrette scowled. "Okay, I'll bite. Is the book missing?"

"It was. Then it was returned. And you know why."

"This I have to hear. Why would anyone take it and bring it back?"

"That was the stumper," Shanks agreed. "But it was also what led straight to you."

"How?" Chet blurted.

"Because whoever stole the book saw some advantage to doing it. And they brought it back because it had already served its purpose, or because they found out their scheme wouldn't work."

"So what purpose was served?" Chet asked.

"None that I could see. So something must have happened between the theft and the return."

"Like what?"

"Look at it this way. If the book hadn't been returned Dixie would have had to call the cops and they would ask to search everyone's cars and suitcases. So how could the thief expect to get the book out of the inn?"

"Good question," said Garrette.

"With an obvious answer. The thief either didn't plan to take the book out or he planned for it to be found. And that only made sense if he expected to put it someone *else's* luggage."

Chet jumped up. *"That's* what changed! The Wahls! The airline lost their luggage."

"Right. But since they arrived during dinner, most people didn't hear about it until Saturday morning. Not long before the book wound up in the pantry." Shanks frowned. "How did you plan to get the book into the Wahls' luggage?"

"I think I know that one," said Chet. "Mr. Garrette asked that the Wahls be put in the room as far away from his as possible. And since he was one of the first people here, we said sure."

For the first time Garrette looked uncomfortable. "Nothing odd about that. I don't like to be anywhere near that man."

"Which is why you keep coming to mystery weekends he'll attend," said Shanks. "I wonder. If we checked with Mr. Lorrel, the owner, do you think it might turn out that you have stayed at this inn before, maybe in the room where the Wahls are now? Those old-fashioned keys wouldn't be hard to get copied."

"Look, what's the point of this? The book was returned, right? No harm, no foul."

Shanks sighed. "There are two problems with that. First, you spoiled my weekend, and I call that a harm. Second, if you get away with this, God knows what you'll try next time. If you hurt somebody I'll have it on my conscience."

Garrette looked shifty. "That Dixie woman won't want let you call the cops."

"She's not my boss. However, I have a two-part plan to avoid such messiness. Chet, can you get some paper and a pen?"

"Right here, sir."

"Excellent. First, Mr. Garrette is going to write a confession. Feel free to explain why you did it—" He figured the man would leap at the chance to unload his complaints about Wahl. "—And if something untoward happens at one of these fiestas with you in attendance it goes to the cops."

Garrette looked grim. "All right. But I'm not going to stop trying to prove he's a crook."

"As long as *you* stay honest that's fine. The second step is simple. You're going to write a check to the charity for what the Hammett book is worth."

Garrette's jaw dropped. "What does that have to with anything?"

"It's a punishment that fits the crime. And the money goes to a good cause."

"I don't have that kind of money to give away!"

Shanks raised an eyebrow. "If you can afford to travel around the country to these circuses you have way too much money, as far as I'm concerned. What do you say, Mr. Garrette? Start writing, or I call the cops."

"What are you up to now, Shanks?" asked Cora. He was on the balcony, writing on a yellow pad.

"Oh. Chet's suddenly taken an interest in mysteries. He wants me to recommend some titles."

She kissed him on his bald spot. "I hope you've included some you didn't write."

"One or two."

"Well, put it down and come to lunch. This is the big finale of the weekend."

Shanks made a face. "Considering that my character is dead wouldn't I be the ghost at the banquet, so to speak?"

"You'll be welcome. Besides, don't you want to know who killed you?"

"Oh, I already do. It was Ross Perry."

"Is that right?" She frowned. "He wasn't supposed to tell."

"He didn't. But when the villain bent down to tap me I smelled Scotch on his breath. Since they served nothing stronger than wine at dinner the only question was who would be carrying a flask."

"Someone who was hiding their drinking. He said he was on the wagon, too. Shanks, you have to talk to him."

"Ross won't listen." He stood up with a sigh. "I suppose I can threaten to haunt him."

True Confession time: I have never been on a murder mystery weekend. I made the whole thing up, and got a whole lot of it wrong.

It gave me a rare chance to tell a fair-play detective story, since the reader knew everything Shanks did. About the theft, that is. I admit I didn't tell you what he was smelling. You can't have everything.

This story appeared in the May 2009 issue of HITCHCOCK'S, ending a three year hiatus by Shanks, the lazy cuss.

SHANKS ON MISDIRECTION

"Just look at him," muttered Leopold Longshanks. "I can't believe he had the gall to show up."

"I'm sure he was invited," said his wife, reasonably. Being reasonable was one of Cora's most annoying habits.

"Well, he *shouldn't* have been," grumbled Shanks. "If there were any justice in the world Ken Roaf would be a pariah. Every cocktail party in the world would bar him from the door. Especially parties given by *writers.*"

"Shanks, it was just a bad review. Get over it." Cora was looking around the living room of Ed and Jean Godwen's huge condo, crammed with partygoers.

"It wasn't just a bad review," said Shanks. "I've had plenty of bad reviews. Well, not as many as *good* ones, of course. But enough to build up a sort of immunity."

"Drinks," said Cora. "There's the bar." She steered towards it and Shanks followed.

The problem wasn't that Ken Roaf had disliked Shanks' new novel. Nor was it that Roaf the oaf, allegedly a friend, had eviscerated the book in a major magazine, while accusing of Shanks of having borrowed too heavily from three long-dead authors.

No. What really stung was that Roaf had gone on to dismiss those three authors – all favorites of Shanks' – as overrated hacks, while declaring that each of them was, nevertheless, far better than Leopold Longshanks. *That* was the straw that had sent the camel to spinal surgery.

After the review appeared Shanks had been unable to write for three days. Instead he glared at the computer screen and muttered:

"Derivative, am I? Uninspired?" until Cora would take him shopping as a punishment.

The bartender informed them that their choices were white wine or red. Shanks couldn't believe it. He had been counting on several Scotches to help him survive an evening under the same roof as Ken Roaf. Instead he was being offered Chardonnay and Merlot.

"You don't have anything stronger?"

The barman looked back, poker-faced. "You mean a fortified wine, like the bums drink? I'm afraid not, sir."

Everyone's a comedian, Shanks thought. Roaf should review *him*.

He looked around the room, Merlot in hand, and wondered if there was anyone here who hadn't seen the review, or at least heard about it. The thing was, no matter how awful the critique is most people seem to stay calm about it – as long as they aren't the one being reviewed. No one seemed ready to ban Roaf from the industry, or even from the party list.

"Stop *looking* for him," said Cora.

"I wasn't. I don't want to see him."

"Shanks, listen to me." She placed herself squarely in front of him. "I won't have you creating a scene. These are our friends."

All except one, he thought.

"Don't start anything with him."

"I'll try to avoid him, my love."

"That's not good enough." She put a hand on his arm and fixed him with her most wifely stare. *"Promise me* you won't say anything harsh to Ken tonight."

"Harsh? *Me?*"

"Promise."

"If Ken behaves himself—"

"Shanks, I am not going to have you embarrass me. If you won't promise right now, I'll take the car and you can find your own way home."

"Now who's being unreasonable?" He sighed. "All right. I promise. No harsh language."

Cora nodded. "Thank you. You'll feel better for it, too. Believe me."

He didn't.

"Oh, there's Jean. I need to say hello. Remember, Shanks—"

"I know, I know." He watched her go and shook his head. It was going to be a long night.

"Shanks! Get over here," called his host. Ed Godwen was the author of bestselling techno-thrillers, a man whose very grocery lists were optioned by Hollywood. He was standing with a couple he introduced as Tom and Maggie Birdeen.

"You write cozies," said Shanks to Maggie, who was fortyish, and whose red hair needed a dye touchup. "I've heard good things about them."

She gave him a very thin smile. "I prefer to say I write traditional, fair play mysteries."

Well, bully for you, Shanks thought. Apparently this was the sort of a night when even polite small talk would get him in trouble. "I've written some of those too," he said.

"Ah," said Maggie Birdeen, plucked eyebrows rising. "Under your own name?" Translation: *I've never heard of you.*

Giving her up as a lost cause, Shanks turned to her husband. "And what do you do, Tom?"

Tom – tall, wiry, with a thin and hungry look, gave him good eye contact and a sincere smile. "I sell insurance, Shanks. It's a pleasure to meet you."

Well, that about completed the set. Shanks discovered, with astonishment, that his wine glass was empty. Maybe he could get over to the bar—

But Ed was talking to him. "How's the new book selling, Shanks?"

Not as well as before Ken Roaf wrote his little tribute, but Shanks had promised not to be harsh. "Not in the same league as yours, I'm sure, but I manage to put a crust on the table."

"What *is* your latest book?" asked Tom, or as Shanks was thinking of him, Mr. Deductable.

Shanks told him the title and Tom frowned. "I read something about that one." He gave him an appraising look.

Shanks sighed.

"I'm afraid I don't have much time to read the bloody potboilers," said Maggie, with a sweet smile. "Just too busy. Busy! We were rushing around so much we almost didn't make it at all tonight."

"Here we go," muttered Tom, who was apparently already tired of this story.

"You see," Maggie told Ed, "we needed money for the sitter and Tom here lost his debit card."

"I didn't *lose* it," said her husband. "The damned ATM *ate* it."

"Ah." Shanks felt unexpected sympathy for the insurance man. All men are brothers before the cruelty of machines. "Did you have trouble with the PIN? If you miss a few times in a row the machine takes the card."

Tom shook his head. "I always type it in right the first time. This machine had just decided to eat *everybody's* card, as the people in front of me had discovered. They just didn't bother to tell me until it was too late."

"Jeez, that was a big help," said Ed.

"Tell us about it," said Shanks.

"I walked up to my usual ATM. It's attached to my bank, so I don't have to pay any fees."

"He walks four blocks to save the two dollar fee," said Maggie. "A lot of good it did him tonight."

"Anyway," said Tom, "there were three Russians standing at the machine."

"Russians?" asked Ed, his techno-thriller instincts alerted.

"Well, Slavic, anyway. And they were speaking one of those eastern European languages. They left the machine and two of them – by the way they were quarreling I assume they were husband and wife—"

"What does *that* mean?" Maggie asked, frowning.

"Just an observation, dear. And the third Russian, a bald guy in one of those black lamb hats, was talking a mile a minute into his cell phone. But none of them had the decency to tell me what was going on. So I put my card into the machine and typed in my code. *Then* they rushed up and told me that the damned thing was eating cards."

"But yours was gone," guessed Ed.

"Call the bank," said Shanks.

"The bank was already closed for the day," said Maggie. "We'll do it first thing in the morning, and Tom can get his card back."

"No," said Shanks. "Call them right now. I mean it. They must have an emergency number for stolen cards."

The three looked at him.

"It wasn't *stolen*," Tom said, slowly, as if explaining to a child. "The machine took it."

"It was *too* stolen," said Shanks, feeling a bit childish himself. "Look, when you walked up to the machine where were the arguing couple?"

Tom thought about it. "On my left, near the wall."

Shanks nodded. "And they were talking loudly, with lots of arm gestures, I'll bet. The bald guy was on your right and behind you."

"That's right." He frowned. "How did you know that?"

"This is Leopold Longshanks," said Ed, with a laugh. "He knows everything. So how does this add up to a theft?"

"While Tom was inserting his card he was distracted by the quarrelers, and didn't notice the bald guy on the other side getting close enough to see him type in the PIN code."

Maggie frowned at her husband. "Is he right?"

Tom scowled. "It doesn't matter. The *machine* got the card."

"Once baldy had the code he signaled to his teammates..." Shanks tried to picture it. "Probably by closing his cellphone. Then they rushed over to warn you about the machine and baldy charged up to try to get your card out."

"But it wouldn't come out," said Tom.

"How do you know?"

"He kept pushing the Eject button again and again."

"Jeez, that's great," said Ed. "The card came out the first time but because he kept hitting the button it *looked* like he couldn't get the card out. Meanwhile it was already in his hand, or on its way to his pocket. Misdirection."

"Exactly," said Shanks. "It's *all* misdirection. Make them look north when the trouble's coming from the south."

"But that's—" Tom blinked. "That's – How could he—"

"You're an idiot," said his wife. "That's how."

"A lot of people get taken that way," said Shanks. "I wish I'd seen it happen."

"What did they get?" asked Ed. "A bank card or a credit card?"

"My debit card." Tom's eyes got wide. "I have to call the company!"

"Good idea," said Shanks. He watched as the insurance man began the cellphone shuffle, wandering around the room looking for better reception.

When he turned around Maggie was staring at him. "How did you know all that?"

"Just part of my research for bloody potboilers."

She made a face. "I'm sorry if I was rude."

Shanks thought it over. "I was too, I guess. It looks like neither of us had a very good day."

"Did you lose a credit card, too?"

"No, it was a bad review."

"Oh." Maggie nodded sympathetically. "I'd rather deal with thieves."

"Amen. Good luck with the bank." Shanks frowned at his empty glass. "I need more wine."

"Should be champagne," said Ed. "To celebrate your latest triumph."

"It *should* be Scotch, but my host doesn't seem to have provided it."

"Jean put the kibosh on that," said Ed. "She says the last time we had a party for writers she had to stop three fist fights and an elopement."

"Oh yes. That was a good party. Wine it is."

There was a free space at the bar for a change. Shanks thought about asking for two glasses. People might think he was carrying one for Cora, but undoubtedly he would run into her and *she* wouldn't be fooled.

"Merlot," he told the bartender.

He turned around and almost bumped into Ken Roaf, the skunk who walked like a man. His so-called friend had the decency to look abashed. Maybe even a little scared, Shanks hoped.

He had sworn to Cora that he would not say anything harsh. But had he promised not to, say, punch anyone? It might be a gray area.

"Uh, Shanks," said Roaf.

"Hello, Ken." And thought: *misdirection.*

He smiled. "Enjoying the party?"

"Uh, yes. Very much. A white wine," he told the bartender.

Shanks looked casually away and, wouldn't you know it, there was his darling wife. Cora was chatting with a publicist and giving Shanks a ferocious glare that said, incongruously, *be nice.*

Oh, he would be *extremely* nice. He just had to figure out how to raise the topic.

Roaf solved that problem. "Uh, Shanks." He cleared his throat. "About that review…"

"Oh, yes," said Shanks. "I'm so glad you brought that up, Ken. I've been meaning to apologize to you for it."

Roaf almost dropped his glass. "*You* want to apologize to *me?*"

"Absolutely. I feel *terrible* about what you've been going through." Shanks shook his head, not so much to show sympathy as to stir his imagination.

"What do you mean?" asked Roaf.

"The things people have been saying about you." Shanks clucked his tongue at the wickedness of slanderers.

"What have they been saying?" Roaf looked just a bit pale.

"I *tell* them and *tell* them. It's because you and I are such good friends that you felt obliged to write that review. You were bending over backwards to be fair."

"That's right, Shanks. That's exactly what I did." Roaf looked at his suddenly empty wine glass. "Another one, please. What do they say after you tell them that?"

"Oh, you know how people talk, Ken. Some people are always willing to assign a malicious motive to the most innocent little action…"

"Like what?" Roaf looked a little glassy-eyed. He frowned at the crowded room. "What are they saying, exactly?"

"Now, there's no point in going into that, Ken. I promised Cora I wouldn't say anything harsh tonight."

"Harsh? They're being *harsh?*"

"Don't dwell on it," Shanks advised. "You and I know you were just trying to tell the truth. Don't we?"

Roaf wandered off, casting suspicious looks at his fellow guests.

Shanks turned back to the bartender, who gave him an equally suspicious glance.

"What was *that* about?"

"Just comforting a friend."

"I spend a lot of time in bars comforting people," the bartender said. "When I'm done they usually look a lot happier than that guy does."

"You have your style, and I have mine. One more glass, please."

Shanks strolled away, admiring the smiling partygoers. Nice crowd.

"There you are!" said Cora. "What did you say to Ken Roaf?"

"Not one harsh word, my love."

"Good for you, Shanks. Now, don't you feel better for that?"

"I suppose I do."

"That Maggie woman told me you were telling her husband not to trust ATM machines. What was that about?"

Was it was worth explaining? Probably not. "What do you think of that dress Maggie's wearing? I don't know much about women's fashion, but…"

"But you're right about that. She should never wear pink."

Shanks sipped wine. Maybe he should start hanging around bank machines. He seemed to have a knack for it.

This story was inspired by two English magazine columnists. Go figure.

John Diamond used to write a weekly piece in the (London) Times Magazine. It was snarkily called "Something For The Weekend," which is UK slang for a condom. One week he cheerfully talked about being a hypochondriac and explained he was going in for a checkup. The next week he announced he had a rare form of tongue cancer (and yes, he was a smoker).

His column then turned into a harrowing, hilarious, look at life in-and-out of cancer therapy. He won the British prize for columnist of the year and wrote two books (C: BECAUSE COWARDS GET CANCER TOO, and SNAKE OIL AND OTHER PREOCCUPATIONS) before the evil bastard got him.

In one of his columns he described an encounter with three Middle Eastern people near an ATM (speaking of evil bastards, come to think of it), and I borrowed his facts for my fiction.

THE SPECTATOR is an English magazine, founded in 1828, and its apparent audience is conservative old-money types. Mary Killen writes an advice column ("Your Problems Solved") in which she gives wildly unusual tips for dealing with problems such as a butler who doesn't serve the beef properly, or the burning question of whether you are expected to chip in for petrol when getting a ride in a private helicopter.

One week a drama critic wrote to say that he had written a play and needed to know how to cope when he ran into fellow critics who had panned it. When I read Killen's advice I thought "I could never do that, but Shanks could," so in this story, he does.

After a three year gap between the last two stories, there was only a one-issue hole between KILLED and MISDIRECTION. Consistency is the hobgoblin of little minds.

SHANKS' GHOST STORY

"I know a ghost story," said Leopold Longshanks. "A true one, too."

"Oh, come on," said Ed Godwen. "You're the biggest skeptic I know. Now you're gonna claim you saw Marie Antoinette's headless body in your hot tub or something?"

Shanks tried for a look of wounded dignity. "This happened many years ago, before I achieved my current level of analytic wisdom."

"Shanks," said Vivian Fanshawe, in her crisp British accent, "you are unbearable sometimes. But do tell your tale."

There were five of them, gathered around the fireplace in the living room of an old Pennsylvania farmhouse. The farm was now owned by an agricultural conglomerate in Nebraska which had no need for quaint farmhouses, and therefore rented it out to people seeking a rural retreat. For half a dozen years a group of writers and spouses had filled the house for a few days around New Year's Eve to catch up with each other and get away from the big parties.

Miles Fanshawe (historical mysteries) was the host this year, and after dinner he had observed that in his native England this was the season for ghost stories.

Personally, Shanks thought that that season should end around age ten, but it was host's privilege, so he had listened politely while Miles recounted a strange event that occurred in his childhood village.

Then Vivian, Miles' wife (children's books), told of the horrifying apparition witnessed by her Aunt Pauline. Finally Ross Perry (spy thrillers) told the shocking tale of a man he had seen peeping on a neighbor, a man who vanished when approached but strongly resembled portraits of the neighbor's dead husband.

Shanks privately attributed the stories to coincidence, hysteria, and, in Ross's case, plain old fiction. But he kept that to himself.

Ed Godwen (techno-thrillers) had denied having any spooky tales to tell. His wife Jean and Shanks' wife Cora were not available to participate, having gone shopping for a New Year's Day luncheon they were planning.

That suited Shanks, who preferred to tell true stories when Cora wasn't available for fact-checking.

"This happened the year my first book was published," he began.

"Just after the invention of movable type," said Ed, cheerfully.

"You should know, since you were in the same rookie class." He paused to plan his narrative. "Well, my novel hadn't set the bestseller list on fire. I was working on the second book as fast as I could, hoping to finish it before circumstances forced me to starve or, worse, get an honest job. Then one day, I got a call from Andy Sutle."

Ross Perry almost choked on his decaf. "My god, I haven't thought of that weasel for years. I think he still owes me money."

"I wouldn't be surprised," said Shanks.

"Who was this gentleman?" asked Vivian.

"He was no gentleman," said Shanks. "He was my first agent, and as slimy as a pit full of used car salesmen."

"I vaguely recall legal proceedings," said Ed. "Did he ever go to jail?"

"Alas, no. He went to Brazil. But his downfall started the very year we are discussing, when Luther Z. Tull filed a lawsuit against him."

"I remember Luther," said Ross. "What a hack. Dabbler in a dozen genres, master of none."

"What was the lawsuit about?" asked Miles.

"Yellow dog contracts," said Shanks. "Andy had realized that the average author could only put out one book a year, but a publisher could put out dozens. So in negotiations he started being more help to the companies than to his clients, with the result that publishers started throwing work his way."

"The weasel," muttered Ross. "But that's not what finished him off. A couple of years later Charlotte Chase Crowe caught his sticky fingers hanging on to the movie money from her romance novels. And unlike Luther she had the dough to hire a good lawyer."

Vivian was frowning. "What does all this have to do with a ghost story? It's just another business scandal."

"Patience, please," said Shanks. "Agent Andy called to ask if I could use some money. He said 'I've got a simple way for you to stretch your skills, make some dough, and impress a big publisher. Have you read Bobby Kingroyal?'"

"More names," complained Miles. "Who's that?"

"For shame," said his wife. "He used to write mysteries set in the American south, dripping with gothic magnolia. Didn't he die a strange death?"

"That's right," said Ross. "His houseboat was found on some river—"

"Sardis Lake," said Shanks.

"Yes. But there was no one on board. Right?"

"Exactly," said Shanks. "And what I'm describing happened just a few months later. Andy told me that Kingroyal had left an outline for his next book. And he, Andy, had talked the publisher into having me finish it, as a work for hire."

"With your name on the cover?" asked Miles.

"Definitely not. All I would get would be the fee. No credit and no publicity. It would appear as Bobby Kingroyal's last book."

"Hold it," said Ed. "I see where this shaggy dog is headed. This is a ghost *writer* story,"

"Is that true?" asked Vivian. "Nothing paranormal, just a free-lance writing job?"

Shanks dropped his bushy eyebrows in a scowl. "You'll have to wait and see. Where did the brandy bottle get to? Thank you, Miles."

"What I don't understand," said Ross, "is why Andy thought of you. Kingroyal's books are all about the Deep South. I mean, have you ever *been* to Mississippi?"

"No, but I have a library card. I borrowed some of his books – his biggest sellers, and some of the recent ones that hadn't done as well – and started through them. Andy sent me the outline and told me to write two sample chapters and a treatment for the rest. Then he said 'Just do it quickly, Shanks, and I'm sure you'll win.'

"That's when I found out I wasn't the only candidate competing for a chance to ghost the novel. They also sent the outline to Thom Willobaugh."

"Well, he's closer geographically, anyway," said Ed. "Didn't he write about Texas?"

"His hero was a private eye in Dallas, I think," Shanks agreed. "I hadn't met the man and didn't care much for his books, so while I hadn't planned to compete, I didn't mind doing so. As long as I won."

"Spoken like a true sportsman," said Ross, frowning at his coffee cup, and at everyone else's brandy glass or beer bottle. He was on the wagon again.

"Long story short, I *did* win, and they gave me six months to produce a bulky Southern gothic blockbuster." He shook his head. "Pretty heady stuff for a guy who had written only one book.

"The first trick was to get the rhythm right. I had a good idea for that; I bought a few audio books of Kingroyal's novels and started playing them in the car and around the house."

"Didn't that annoy Cora?" asked Vivian.

"Hadn't met her yet. I kept them playing all the time, not in order and not even the same book. I didn't need a plot; I just wanted to immerse myself in his *language*."

"Clever," said Ed. "But not yet spooky."

"I'm getting there. It happened on the fifth day of writing. I was feeling good; I had finally gotten into the zone."

There were murmurs of appreciation. "I *love* that," said Miles. "When the book is working perfectly, and food and sleep became *irritants*."

"And the characters start speaking to you," said Ross, with a dreamy smile.

Shanks considered chatting with your characters a sign of creeping schizophrenia, but to each his own. "I remember calling Andy when I broke for lunch and telling him that the book was really beginning to move. But later, just as dusk was falling and I was about to start chapter seven, set in a swamp outside Pascegoula, the phone rang. I picked it up and heard an unfamiliar voice. It was high-pitched and whiny, with a hint of a southern accent.

"'You can't do this,' it said.

"'Excuse me?' I replied.

"'You're stealing my work, Longshanks. I won't let you do it.'

"'Who the hell is this?'

"'I won't let you write my book. This is worse than plagiarism; it's identity theft. It's *evil*.' Then he hung up."

"Now we're getting to it," said Vivian, with a happy shiver. "Did it sound like Bobby Kingroyal?"

"Beats me. I had never heard his voice. He didn't record his own audio books and this was before there were recordings of every public figure on the Web."

"I love those," said Ed. "Watching politicians say stupid things is my new hobby."

"That call must have been disturbing," said Miles.

"You can say that again," said Shanks. "It ended my work for the day. I started thinking about who had a motive for wanting me to fail."

"Thom Willobaugh," said Ross instantly. "You beat him for the right to ghost the book. Of course he held a grudge."

"That was my first thought," Shanks agreed. "I spent the rest of the evening calling friends, tracking down his unlisted number.

"I reached him the next day and we chatted for a while. He was clearly annoyed about losing and we commiserated about being thrown into competition unknowingly."

"Was he the voice on the phone?" asked Vivian.

"I couldn't tell. His voice was deeper, and he had no accent. Of course, it would make sense for him to disguise it, wouldn't it? But we had a good conversation and my conclusion was, if he was the caller, I didn't think he'd be doing it again."

"How come I didn't hear about all this back then?" asked Ed.

"You had just stolen Jean away from me, remember? We weren't on the best of terms."

"What can I say?" said Ed. "The best man won."

"Not the most modest one, apparently."

"More importantly," said Ross. "Why didn't you tell the weasel?"

Shanks shrugged. "Embarrassment, really. Remember, I had only written one book. I was afraid Andy Sutle would think I was trying to get out of the deal."

"More likely," said Miles, "he would have thought you'd gone round the twist. Bonkers.""So, what did you do next?" asked Vivian.

"What could I do? I went back to work." Shanks frowned. "Of course, the writing didn't go as well. I felt like someone was looking over my shoulder the whole time.

"I remember I went to the library one day to research a locale for one of the big scenes and found myself looking up the details of Bobby Kingroyal's death."

"To make sure he hadn't pulled an Elvis," said Ross.

"They never did find his body," said Vivian. "Bobby's, I mean."

"Alligators," said Ed, with the smile of a man plotting his next book.

"Believe me," said Shanks. "I was aware that his body had never turned up. It took another week before I had the rhythm back. Andy was calling every other day, wanting progress reports, telling me he had gone to bat for me, and I had better not fail him."

"I really *loathe* that weasel," said Ross.

"So one evening, just as I was quitting for the day, the phone rang. I assumed it was Andy again. But it was that other voice."

"From beyond the grave," said Miles, appreciatively. "Or at least, beyond Sardis Lake."

"He said 'You can't steal a man's life like this, Longshanks. You can't rob me of everything I've worked for. Everything I am.'

"I said: 'Mr. Kingroyal, is that you?'"

"He laughed. 'What's left of me. And you're trying to steal it. Tell those bastards you won't do it. No good can come of this.'"

"Ah, a threat," said Ross, with satisfaction. "I was wondering when we'd come to that."

"Did you try Star 69?" asked Ed.

"Yes, but it was blocked. I ordered caller I.D., but by the time it was set up it was too late."

"Did you finish the book?" asked Miles.

"Finally." Shanks shook his head. "The last few weeks were a nightmare. I threw out all those audiotapes. I didn't want to hear Kingroyal's words anymore. I wanted that man out of my head forever. Out of my *life*. Is there any brandy left?"

"I'll be mother," said Miles, reaching for the bottle. "Anyone else?" The only reply was a mournful sigh from Ross.

"One bright summer morning I called Andy and told him the book was done, and I was sending it by messenger. That afternoon the mysterious caller rang back."

"I'm guessing he was cranky," said Ed.

"He said 'You think you're a ghostwriter, Longshanks, but you aren't a ghost. You're a vampire, a ghoul. You sucked my blood, drained my life away. Do you think you can get away with that?'"

"Oh my," said Vivian. "Quite the poor loser."

"What happened next?" asked Miles.

Shanks' eyebrows rose. "Not much, really. The publisher approved the book, paid my fee, and put it out as the last, great Kingroyal. It sold better than his last few novels, I'm proud to say."

"That was because it was his last book," said Ross. "Attracted the morbid."

"Very possibly. Anyway, I never heard from the mystery caller again."

"Do you think it was his ghost?" asked Vivian.

"Ectoplasm doesn't make phone calls," said her husband, firmly. "I still think it was the rival for the book contract. What was his name? Willobaugh. Writers can be spiteful, heaven knows."

"I'm guessing it was Kingroyal," said Ed, "but he was alive and calling from whichever rehab or brothel he was hiding out in."

"It was Andy Sutle," said Ross.

"What possible motive would the agent have?" asked Vivian.

"Didn't need one, the little weasel. Did I mention he owes me money? Besides, have you noticed the calls came right after Shanks reported progress to Andy? How did the ghost know about that?"

"Jeez, Shanks," said Ed. "Is that really all? It's not like you to tell a story without an ending."

"Thanks for noticing. That's why I don't write mainstream fiction."

Shanks savored a sip of brandy. "There *is* a sort of postscript. Two years later I attended a mystery convention and one panel featured a writer with a high-pitched, whiny voice and a slight southern accent."

"Willobaugh?" guessed Miles.

"Kingroyal in disguise," said Ed.

"None of the above," said Shanks. "It was Luther Z. Tull."

There was a moment of silence. Finally Ross said: "The hack? The guy who sued Andy Sutle?"

"None other. I bought him a drink after the panel and he confessed. He had made the calls."

"For heaven's sake, why?" asked Miles.

"Because he wrote the outline I was working from. You see, I really *was* stealing his work. Luther had written the last three Bobby Kingroyal novels."

"But the man was still alive when those books came out!" said Ed.

"Alive, but not writing. Luther told me that five years earlier Bobby had told the publisher 'a moderately trained monkey could write my books. Find one and just send me the royalties.'"

"How sad," said Vivian.

"Very. I think he was heavily into the booze by then."

"I'll bet the mysterious death was a suicide," said Miles. "Poor drunken sod."

Ross hugged his coffee cup to his chest. "It's terrible when people lose control like that."

"True," said Shanks. "Luther told me that when he started, he asked Bobby for advice. Kingroyal said 'just update *Gone With The Wind,* add progressive politics and kill someone on page one. The proles eat it like candy.'"

Ed snorted. "He knew his audience, I'll say that for him."

"Anyway, when Luther filed suit against Andy he had no idea how much influence Andy had with the publisher. They took the deal away from him. Luther was heartbroken. These books were the only things he ever wrote that hit the bestseller list, even if they did have someone else's name on the cover. Naturally he hated to see me writing the next one, especially from his outline. By the way, there was someone at the publisher who felt Luther had gotten a raw deal, and she kept him up to date about my progress."

"Why didn't he tell you about what was going on when he called you?" asked Ross. "Hell, why didn't he tell the world? I would have."

"He said the contract had confidentiality pledges with penalties he couldn't afford to pay, and I'm sure that was true. *Mine* threatened me with everything except plagues of locusts. But I think there was another reason. Luther had been pretending to be Bobby Kingroyal for almost five years. He couldn't bring himself to step out from behind the curtain."

"You realize what this means?" said Ed. "I was right. This wasn't a ghost story at all. You cheated us, Shanks."

"That's true!" said Miles. "You promised something spooky, not just another sordid tale of the publishing trade."

"You want spooky?" Shanks leaned forward, bushy eyebrows dropping in a menacing scowl. "How about this? I received *three* of those phone calls, but Luther swore up and down that *he only made two of them.*"

Vivian's eyes went wide. "Gosh! Really?"

"No," said Shanks.

The idea for this story came to me when we were volunteering at an archaeological dig at Ramat Rachel in Israel. (Great fun, but hard on the back muscles.) Why middle-eastern heat brought Pennsylvania winter to mind is one of those minor mysteries.

I should explain that I hate and despise the storytelling trick I call "Ooh, spooky." That can be defined as follows: a story has a supernatural element which is dispelled with a materialistic explanation. Then, at the last minute, it is brought back purely for effect. "But if you didn't light up the painting and I didn't either — Then there really was a ghost! Ooh, spooky!" For some reason TV movies are especially susceptible to it.

Like I said, I hate that. So I set one up and had Shanks shoot it down. This is the first appearance of this story.

SHANKS' MARE

"My company makes ticketing systems for concert halls and similar venues," said Peter Bitrun. "We don't have much experience with horse theft."

Leopold Longshanks nodded gravely. "It doesn't seem to be a big problem in New York City these days."

"So why do you think we would be concerned with this particular ... uh, caper?" Bitrun sat back comfortably in his desk chair, which could have held a family of four. He was in his early sixties, with distinguished gray hair and piercing eyes. Any movie studio would have happily cast him as a corporate president, which, in fact, is what he was.

"And if I may ask, Mr. Longshanks—"

"Call me Shanks."

"Why are you the one investigating? If I understood correctly, you're a novelist." His tone suggested that the word was synonymous with *hobo.*

"Believe me," said Shanks, "I wish the police were here instead, but Polly Ellinger says no, and she's the one who owns the horse, and the stable where it happened."

He dropped a photocopy onto Bitrun's hardwood desk. "This is what she found tacked to the door of Misty's stall this morning."

> IF YOU WANT THIS HORSE BACK
> GET $25,000 READY
> CALL THE COPS SHE DIES

Bitrun's mouth formed an astonished O. "That's a lot of money. Is the horse worth that?"

That was exactly what Shanks had asked Polly when she had called him and his wife early that morning and begged them to rush over. Cora and Polly shared a favorite charity and had spent many happy hours together gouging money out of people for a good cause.

"Of *course* Misty isn't worth it," Polly had said. She was a handsome woman in her fifties. Her brunette hair swelled in an elaborate 'do', as usual. The three of them had been sitting in her kitchen, drinking coffee and staring at the ransom note.

"I just heard about a horse," said Cora. "It sold for—"

"Those are thoroughbreds. *Racehorses.*" Polly shook her head. "Mine are grade horses. They're for giving kids riding lessons, not for racing. They have to be calm and easy-going, the exact opposite of those neurotic prima donnas that go off at five-to-one in the Daily Double."

"Do you think they were looking for Misty? Or was she chosen at random?"

"She was the target," said Shanks. "I took a look at the stable before we came in here. Misty's stall is in the middle."

Cora frowned. "So?"

"So if you were taking just any horse and you wanted to be safe you'd pick the one farthest from the house. It's a shorter distance to the road and less risk that Polly would hear something. If they wanted to show off, they'd choose the horse *closest* to the house. Besides—" He pointed at the note. "It says *she* so they knew they were after a mare."

Polly smiled. "You see, Cora? We don't need the cops. Shanks can find Misty."

"Now what a minute," said Shanks, while his wife shook her head.

"He's a mystery writer," said Cora, "not a detective. Half the time he can't find his car keys."

"Don't help," he muttered.

But Polly won, and here he was.

"I still don't see how this involves my company," said Bitrun.

"We have to assume that the horse thieves expected to get something out of the deal," said Shanks. "Since the mare isn't worth anything like the amount they demanded either the purpose was to upset Polly—"

"And damage her business."

"Right. Or maybe the ransom note was misdirection, and there was something else to be gained by taking the horse. So I asked whether Misty had any regular customers, so to speak."

"Oh yes," said Polly. "She's extremely popular. An easy ride and maybe the calmest horse I've got. If you're high-strung yourself it can be a wonderful thing to work with a relaxed animal." She looked Shanks up and down. "You know, *you* could use a little stress relief, not to mention exercise."

"Now, wait a minute."

"I don't know about stress," said Cora. "If he got any more relaxed he'd be limp. But you're right about the exercise."

"Did Misty have any regulars?" Shanks asked. They weren't getting him up on one of those things.

"That's what I'm getting at. Jessica Folie was supposed to have her lesson on Misty today, before school, and by the time I thought to call them they were on their way and I didn't have her cell number." Polly shook her head at the memory. "That poor kid."

"What's her problem?" asked Cora.

"She's one of those teens headed for total collapse before she gets out of high school," said Polly. "Her parents are already trying to decide which Ivy League college she'll attend. So all of her supposed spare time is spent building up a resumé to impress admissions officers."

"I've heard about this," said Cora. "It's not enough to get good grades and test scores anymore. The kids have to put in hours of community service, and have prize-winning hobbies."

"Exactly," said Polly. "That poor child doesn't have a minute to herself. When she isn't doing homework, she's playing violin in the town orchestra, or volunteering in a soup kitchen, for Pete's sake."

"How does horseback riding fit in?" asked Shanks.

"It doesn't. Oh, I've heard her mother on the phone, bragging about Jessica like she's going to the Olympics, but the girl is in it just for fun. I think her therapist suggested it; he's sent other kids to me." Polly ran a hand through her hairdo. "Sometimes when her parents don't stay for the lesson she doesn't even ride, just spends the hour talking to Misty and grooming her. That's her idea of *rebellion*."

"How did Jessica take it when she found out Misty was gone?"

Polly shuddered. "Ever see a teenager have a nervous breakdown?"

"Seriously?" asked Cora.

"I don't know what else to call it. Not a tantrum; just weeping and shaking. Apparently she's taking some pre-college test this weekend and an hour of riding was supposed to be her big chance to unwind."

"And now she going to be worried about the horse," said Cora. "Instead of studying. The poor thing."

"Ms. Folie couldn't calm her daughter down. She finally had to call her husband, which she did *not* want to do. I guess he's better at talking to Jessica, because it seemed to work."

"Tell me about the father," Shanks said.

"He's a big executive at some company in the city. A dedicated parent, I guess, but just as ambitious as his wife. If Jessica doesn't win at least one Nobel Prize by the age of thirty those two are going to be seriously ticked off."

"If he's such a good dad, why didn't the mother want to call?"

"Apparently this is a big day for him. His company is working on a huge deal and he's the point man. His wife said today could make or break his career."

"Ah," said Shanks.

"Ah," said Bitrun. "You think the horse theft might have something to do with Mike Folie and our big project."

Shanks shrugged. "It seemed worth checking out. And since I couldn't speak to Mr. Folie by phone—"

"At his own request. He asked that we hold his calls so he can concentrate." Bitrun sighed. "Look, Mr. Longshanks, we've been working for months on a chance to set up a major partnership with a Japanese company. All my top people are involved, but Mike is running it."

He smiled wryly. "Frankly, one reason for that is that he's my only department head who speaks Japanese. But he *is* my star player, you might say. I fully expect him to take my place when I retire."

"And today is important?" Shanks asked.

"Crucial. Each of the competing companies has one last chance for a live video presentation to the corporate executives in Tokyo. Mike will be making our case."

"Not a good time to be distracted."

"Definitely not." Bitrun's brow wrinkled in concentration. "I suppose one of our competitors might be that unscrupulous."

That's one possibility, Shanks thought. But there were others.

Mike Folie was pushing fifty. By the look of it, he was pushing his blood pressure too. He had the wide eyes and short breath of a fanatic, and it turned out that the Japanese project had been his idea.

"I can do this, Peter," he told his boss. "Don't worry. I won't let anything distract me."

"I know, Mike," said Bitrun, patting him on the shoulder. "We're all counting on you."

"We have no choice," said a nasal voice.

Shanks turned and saw two newcomers. The speaker was introduced as Jon Dillon. His narrow eyes and pointy nose made Shanks think of something reptilian.

The other new arrival was a woman named Nadine Tana. She was dressed in the best fashion of a rising New York executive, and spoiled – or completed? – the look with a pair of spinsterish eyeglasses on a chain. The spectacles came across as a note of defiant nonconformity, like a flower pinned to a uniform.

"This is the rest of my Tokyo team," Bitrun explained. He listed the job titles of the newcomers but the corporate-babble went right past Shanks.

"One of Nadine's specialties is scouting the competition," the boss added. "She can give you a list of our rivals."

Shanks pulled out his ever-present pocket notebook. "Could you e-mail it to Sam Piper at this address? He's the only one at the stables who knows computers. He'll print out the list and see if any names ring a bell there. They might be on the customer list, or among the neighbors."

Tana looked at the page over the top of her glasses. Shanks never saw her look through them. "I'll have my secretary take care of it right away."

"Great," said Bitrun. "Is there anything else we can do for you, Mike?"

"I wonder," said Shanks, mildly. "Can anyone think of someone *else* who might want Mr. Folie to fail?"

Then he dearly wished he had a video camera. The next ten seconds were a master class in non-vocal communication.

Tana was halfway to the door with the list. She froze in place for a moment. Then she turned and stared directly at Dillon, who gazed right back. His narrow eyes were reduced to slits.

Bitrun was frowning at both of them, and Folie – well, he looked like a man who had suddenly discovered he was standing in a room full of rattlesnakes.

Tana and Dillon – the other members of the elite Tokyo Team – each had reason to want Mike to fail. Mike, the man Bitrun said was likely to be the next president of the company.

And now each of them suspected the other one of horse-napping – or was pretending to. *Interesting.*

"I can't think of anyone," said Bitrun, firmly.

Clearly no one was going to disagree with the boss. Tana nodded and left to make the arrangements.

Dillon shook his head. "Mike, we still need to go over those software options."

Folie blinked. "Right. Let's do it." He looked at Shanks. "You'll let me know if you hear anything?"

"Absolutely." He watched them go. Shanks was glad his job didn't depend on that poor guy getting everything right today.

"He's crazy about his daughter, Mr. Longshanks," said Bitrun, back behind his desk now. "A good father. This is hard on him."

"You're very understanding."

Bitrun rubbed his chin. "My wife died of an aneurysm six months after our wedding. That was the day I stopped panicking over little things. There's always another business deal."

Shanks wondered whether he should bluntly ask whether someone within the company might have wanted to see Folie fail.

But Bitrun had other things on his mind. "It's almost time for the video conference with Tokyo. It's quite fascinating. Mike sits in a room with the camera. I sit on the other side of a glass wall with Nadine, Jon and a translator who tries to tell us what's going on. The four of us could probably accomplish more by playing bridge, but it feels like we ought to be participating."

"What time is it in Japan?"

"Before breakfast. But that company likes to show off that they can deliver 24/7. The global economy thing."

It sounded like it might be worth seeing, for entertainment value, at least, but Shanks couldn't think of a way to wangle an invitation. Instead he took an elevator down to the street and ordered a late lunch at a steak house. While waiting for his main course he called the stable and heard a report of no progress.

"Polly is pretty morose," Cora told him. "I'm contemplating getting her drunk."

"I'll leave that to your wise judgment."

"Thanks a heap. Did Mr. Folie have any idea who might have done this?"

"Still working on it, love. Keep trying to convince Polly to call the cops."

"Hmm. Maybe a few drinks would help with that. You aren't breaking your diet in the big city, are you, Shanks?"

"As a matter of fact, I just finished a salad," he said, which was true. The waiter was clearing away the green stuff to make room for some medium rare sirloin.

After lunch he returned to the reception room at Bitrun's firm and made more phone calls.

Then he paused. Polly had said Misty was a bay mare, and he had just realized he had no idea what "bay" meant. Was it a color like chestnut, or a breed like palomino?

Discovering he was using a word he couldn't define annoyed him, like a carpenter opening his tool box and finding a gadget he didn't recognize. Borrowing a dictionary from the receptionist Shanks determined that a bay horse is reddish-brown, with black mane and tail. It didn't help find Misty, but it made him feel he'd accomplished something.

He spent a while thinking about his next novel. Maybe his husband-and-wife team could go undercover to investigate corporate espionage.

The notebook came out and he had just started jotting down some ideas when Sam Piper called again.

Almost two hours passed before most of the Tokyo Team returned, cheerful as could be. Mike Folie wasn't with them.

Shanks stood up. "How'd it go?"

"Very well," said Bitrun. "Mike came through like a trooper."

"He blew the Korean options," said Dillon.

"That was the material *you* briefed him on, wasn't it?" said Tana, with a sweet smile.

Bitrun shook his head tolerantly, like a man surrounded by bickering children. "Any news, Mr. Longshanks?"

"I'm afraid so. I'd like to get some advice from the three of you."

Bitrun ushered them into his office. "You sound like it's bad news."

"It is." Shanks sighed. "Sam called from the stables. There's no word from the thieves but Polly just realized that Misty was due for a dose of medicine this morning."

"Vitamins?" asked Dillon.

"Nothing that simple, I'm afraid. Misty has some chronic condition. Sam told me the name but it meant nothing to me."

"Is it bad?" asked Tana.

"From what I understand damn near anything that goes wrong with a horse can kill it," said Shanks. "But the mare will be all right if she gets her dose of this veterinary drug—" He tore another page from his notebook and dropped it on the conference table. "Tryfino Gold. Otherwise she could be dead by morning."

"Man." Dillon's lips pierced. "How do you dispose of a dead horse?"

They all stood for a moment, pondering that one.

"And how will Mike tell his daughter?" Tana asked. "Oh, this is going to be hard."

"That's my question to you," said Shanks. "I think we have to tell Mr. Folie, so he can decide on what to say to his daughter. Who should talk to him?"

Shanks could have heard a pin drop, or at least a lot of throats being cleared.

Finally Bitrun spoke. "You seem to be doing so well with Mike, Shanks. Why don't you tell him? Rather than him getting it second hand, so to speak."

The others rushed to agree and Dillon even offered to walk him down to Folie's office.

"I'm sorry you've had to waste your whole day on this," said Dillon. "I've never seen someone get so worked up about a pony."

"A horse his daughter cares about," Shanks noted.

"Yeah. If you ask me that kid of his is spoiled rotten. All those extras he gives her. French lessons, orchestra, tennis—"

"Is that spoiled? Sounds more like overworked to me."

Dillon snorted. "She doesn't know what overwork is. Never worked for Peter Bitrun. Here's Mike's office. Good luck."

Folie was busy at his computer. He looked up eagerly. "Any news?"

"Not really," said Shanks. "How did the interview go?"

"Very well. There are two other companies in the race, and one of them may beat us, but we did our best." He sighed. "I just talked to my wife. We're trying to figure out what to do if the horse never comes back. We'll buy Jessica one of her own and she'll just have to get over the loss, I guess."

"Kids bounce back."

"They have to, don't they? Let me finish this memo and we can talk."

Ten minutes later Shanks' phone rang. "Hey, Sam. Good to hear from you."

He scribbled notes while Mike Folie watched wide-eyed. "News?"

"Maybe. Could you call Mr. Bitrun and ask if we can come back over there?"

Folie's face went red. "You think it was one of my co-workers, don't you? Stabbing me in the back?"

"We'll know more soon. Who's in charge of computers here?"

He blinked at the change of subject. "Our Chief Information Officer?"

"That's too high up the food chain. I mean someone who knows where all the bytes are buried."

"Oh. The systems manager?"

"Sounds about right. Call him up and ask him to come along."

He turned out to be a *she,* named Jackie Houchin. She was a thirty-ish beanpole with stop-sign-red hair and two visible tattoos.

When the three of them reached the president's office they found the rest of the Tokyo Team looking at some documents.

Bitrun was the first to notice. "Ah, Mike. Any news?"

"I have some," said Shanks.

"I'm sorry," said Tana, "but I really don't see what this alleged horse theft has to do with our company. Peter, we have to settle these proposals."

"She's right," said Dillon. "No offense, Mike, but this is getting tiresome."

Even Bitrun looked irritated, as if he were trying to find a polite way to tell Folie to get back to work.

Shanks said: "I've been lying to you."

Well, *that* got their attention.

It was the perversity of human nature, he mused. Write a novel and people want to know who each character is *really* based on. And a boring fact becomes fascinating when it turns out to be a falsehood.

Dillon shook his head. "What lie? You mean the horse wasn't stolen?"

"Oh, she was stolen, and she's still missing," said Shanks. "But remember when I asked Ms. Tana to send an email to Sam at the stable?"

"The list of our competitors." said Bitrun.

"Exactly. That was a lie. Sam doesn't work at the stable. He's the webmaster at my publisher."

Dillon frowned. "If this is industrial sabotage it's pathetic. You could pick up that list from a trade magazine."

"Believe me, Sam didn't want the list. He threw it out immediately. All he cared about was the address it came from."

They were all frowning now, except Jackie. For the first time the systems manager seemed interested.

"You see," said Shanks. "Driving over here it occurred to me that some rival of Mike's in the company might have taken the horse to throw him off his game."

"This is slander," said Dillon.

"Then you have plenty of witnesses. How about letting me dig myself in deeper?"

"Please do," said Bitrun. He was seated behind the desk with fingers steepled, like a judge about to make a tough decision.

"I suggested to Sam that I would tell the suspects – no offense – that Misty was sick and needed a dose of medicine."

"I *thought* that was awfully convenient," said Tana.

"So you say now," snapped Shanks, bushy eyebrows dropping into a scowl. She reminded him of certain book reviewers.

"Wait a minute," said Mike. "Are you saying Misty is not only missing, but *sick?*"

"Try to keep up," grumbled Dillon. "He's saying he lied about that. Your precious horse is fine."

"As far as we know," Shanks clarified. "Anyway, I asked Sam to make up a webpage for a non-existent veterinary drug, so that if the horse thief looked it up—Jackie, you're shaking your head."

Her bright red hair was practically vibrating. "Wouldn't work. It takes a while for the search engines to find a new web page."

"That's exactly what Sam said. But he pointed out that my publisher had what he called a teaser page for a new novel that will be out in a few months. All it says is *'Tryfino Gold* is coming.'"

Shanks shrugged. "As a matter of fact, that's the title of my next book. Pretty soon the webpage will have information about it, but now it's essentially blank. However, it's been around long enough for the search engines to find it."

"I get it," said Jackie, grinning. "You had Nadine send the message to your webmaster so he would have the IP range."

"IP range?" Bitrun frowned. "What range is that?"

"Computer addresses," said Shanks. "As I understand it every computer attached to the web has its own IP address. Companies buy ranges of them, so all the machines in one firm tend to have similar numbers. Once Sam received that email from Ms. Tana's secretary all he had to do was watch the Tryfino Gold page to see if someone from a similar address looked for it."

"That's cool," said Jackie.

"Glad you like it. Here's the interesting part. Mike, fifteen minutes after I told your co-workers that the horse needed a dose of Tryfino Gold, someone from this company went looking for that product on the web."

Dillon aimed a wolfish smile at Tana. "Well, well."

"Don't look at *me*," she said, glaring back.

With what he hoped was a dramatic flourish, Shanks tore another page from his notebook. "Here's the address the viewer used. If Jackie will check the number we'll know whose computer—"

"That's enough," said Bitrun. He was on his feet, and red in the face.

Everyone turned to stare at him.

"I'll be damned," muttered Dillon.

Mike Folie looked ready to weep. "Peter? It was *you?*"

"What gives?" asked Jackie.

"Everyone get out of here," said Bitrun. "Everyone but Mike."

Jackie was still asking for an explanation. Nadine Tana took her by the arm and steered her towards the door.

"Shanks stays," said Folie. "He has a right to know what's going on. And so do I."

The president sat on the edge of his desk and folded his arms. Shanks thought he looked irritated more than anything else. "You're assuming I had something to do with that damned horse. I haven't said so."

"Don't insult my intelligence, Peter. Are you telling me you won't let Jackie check the web address because it might turn out to be Jon or Nadine's computer? No, it was *you*." He shook his head. "My God. I just remembered your lodge in Sussex County. That's only about an hour from the stable. I'll bet that's where you've got Misty."

"Look," said Bitrun, "I promise you your horse is perfectly safe."

"Give me a reason, Peter. For heaven's sake, why would you want to make my daughter miserable and endanger the Tokyo deal?"

"I think I know," said Shanks. "Your boss told me he expected you to replace him when he retired. I guess he thought you were moving up too fast."

"You don't know a damned thing," said Bitrun. "I *want* to retire. I'm looking forward to it."

"Then *why?*" Folie repeated.

Bitrun sighed. "I've spent more than thirty years building up this company, Mike. I can't leave unless I know it's in good hands."

"Oh, for god's sake." Folie turned to look at Shanks. "Do you get it? He thinks my love for my family is *weakness.*"

"Be sensible, Mike."

"Did he tell you that his wife died just after their wedding?"

"He mentioned it," Shanks said.

"He usually does. Did he tell you he was back at his desk the day after the funeral? Peter thinks a man who cares too much about his family is unfit to command."

"He's blowing this out of proportion," said Bitrun, looking to Shanks for support.

"This was the final test, wasn't it?" asked Folie. "In order to succeed you I had to prove that I could do my job when my family was in trouble. And to my everlasting shame, I passed with flying colors."

To Shanks, Bitrun seemed equal parts concerned and confused, as if he understood that Folie was upset but couldn't figure out why. "You should be proud of the job you did today. I know I am. I can retire happily now, knowing the company is in good hands."

"I quit," said Folie.

Bitrun jerked back as if he'd been slapped. "You can't!"

"I just did. How can I work for you after this, Peter? Tell him, Shanks."

How did I become the referee? Shanks wondered. "Don't quit now. Take a day to think about it."

"Why should I?"

Shanks thought fast. "You don't want your daughter believing it's her fault you're out of a job, do you?"

Folie frowned. "That's ridiculous."

"Sure it is. But a lot of kids think it's their fault when their parents get divorced. And that's ridiculous too, isn't it?"

"He's right," said Bitrun, soothingly. "Just sleep on it, Mike. It'll all feel different in the morning."

As if that problem were solved, he turned to Shanks, eyes narrowing shrewdly. "What do I have to do to keep this quiet, Mr. Longshanks?"

You have to admire his nerve, Shanks thought. *Like it's just another business deal.*

"What about the rest of your team? They know – or surely suspect – what happened."

"They work for me. I'll handle them. But what about *you?*"

Shanks shook his head. "I can't even think about that, Mr. Bitrun, until two things happen."

"Name them."

"First, you have to call Polly Ellinger and tell her where to find the horse, safe and sound."

"No problem. Give me her number."

Shanks tore another page from his sadly depleted notebook. "Also on that page is the name of a charity. You're going to make out a certified check to them. Your own funds, not the company's."

"How much?"

"Twenty-five thousand dollars."

Bitrun blinked. "That's a hell of a lot of money."

"It sure is," Shanks agreed. "You picked it."

"So it is. Very well, I agree to your conditions." Bitrun picked up the phone. "Give me some privacy, please."

Folie was ready to stay and argue but Shanks took him by the arm. "Let's get the horse back, Mike."

They went past the secretary's desk and into the empty hallway. Folie turned to scowl at Shanks. "I can't believe you want to let him get away with this!"

"I don't. Once the mare is safe and the check clears I'll call the cops."

"But you promised that you wouldn't."

"No, I said I wouldn't consider making such a promise until we had the check and the horse."

Folie thought that over. "Why is he giving the money to charity, if not to buy silence?"

"Public relations, I assume. He's going to need all the good will he can get." Shanks patted Folie on the shoulder. "And the company is going to need a new leader. That's why I didn't want you to quit."

"This is incredible. How can I ever thank you?"

"Since you mention it, there is a way."

Folie looked suddenly wary. Shanks didn't blame him.

"Your daughter's name is Jessica, right?"

"Yes. What about her?"

"Let her drop one extracurricular activity of her choice."

Folie thought about it. His face turned red. "You have no right to ask that!"

"True," said Shanks. "But you asked how you can repay me, and that's how. If you refuse, well—"

He shrugged. "We'll both know you're an ingrate, that's all."

"You don't know anything about my daughter. How can you claim to know she's working too hard?"

"I think *all* the kids being pushed into Ivy League schools are worked too hard. Your daughter is the only one I can do something about."

Folie sighed and shook his head. "I'll talk to her. But don't be surprised if she says no. She's pretty ambitious."

"That's all I ask."

"What do you expect her to do with this free time if she gets it?"

"Whatever fifteen year old girls do these days, I suppose. Watch bad TV. Gossip about boys. Maybe read a book that isn't on some recommended list."

Shanks brightened. "I'll send you a copy of Tryfino Gold. The advance blurbs have been pretty good."

You might think that this story started with the title. (SHANK'S MARE is an old term for traveling by foot.) You'd be wrong.

My first series character was Marty Crow, a private eye who lived in Atlantic City and was a compulsive gambler. I got the idea of having him involved with a stolen race horse, but I was having better luck selling stories about Shanks, so I made a transfer.

Jon Dillon is actually the name of a co-worker of mine who knows a lot more about computers than I do. He gave me some advice about the technical bits of this story.

Jackie Houchin, on the other hand, I have never met, but there is a real person of that name, and she was kind enough to offer me some advice about horses.

I thank the real Jon and Jackie for their help and their willingness to let me borrow their names. They had to wait quite a while for the privilege, because this story was rejected by the magazines. Of course, all mistakes are my own, so don't blame Jackie and Jon.

SHANKS FOR THE MEMORY

"We've lived here too damned long," said Leopold Longshanks.

Awkward silence told him he had spoken a little too forcefully. Perhaps he hadn't needed that last glass of wine.

"Come on, Shanks," said Cora, his wife. "You *love* this town."

"It's a nice little place," said Jennifer. She was a wide-eyed blonde, in her late twenties, and she had sparked Shanks' outburst by asking how long they had lived here.

"Feeling a little claustrophobic?" asked Ronnie. "I can't blame you. Life in suburbia would drive me nuts. But then, I'm southern California born and bred."

And that was exactly why this foursome had gathered. Ronnie was a movie agent – a person who attempted to sell literary works to the studios – and the natural habitat of such creatures was L.A., just as book agents tended to wither away if removed from Manhattan.

After nearly thirty years of being a published author Shanks had grown tired of the shortage of insulting offers from Hollywood. He was eager to sell out and have more of his works butchered in return for easy money, so he had decided to add a second agent to his quiver.

Ronnie was the only one who had risen to the bait so far. His response took the form of a suggestion that when he and his companion next visited the Big Apple they would venture over the bridge for a dinner meeting.

Shanks knew better than to get his hopes up, but he was only human. Even the sight of Ronnie – terminally tan, impossibly young – hadn't dashed his hopes.

Dinner conversation took care of that.

"Mysteries are dead, Shanks," Ronnie had announced over *saag paneer* at the Big Bombay. "Nobody wants to see someone solve a crime anymore, because no one believes that crimes get solved."

"They don't?"

"Not by *people*," Ronnie explained, reaching for another piece of naan. "Crimes get solved by gadgets now – forensic stuff – or by guns. Not brains. That's what the public thinks, so that's what they want to see."

"What I like," bubbled Jennifer, "is thrillers." She had introduced herself as an actress, but the word that occurred to Shanks was *starlet*.

"Yeah," said Ronnie. "Suspense. That's what the studios want, Shanks. Not heroes chasing bad guys. Bad guys chasing heroes. Do you have any books like that?"

"He does," said Cora. She seemed to be enjoying the evening a little too much, possibly because she already had a movie agent for her romance novels. "But nobody likes them as much as his mysteries, including him. Shanks still thinks the human brain can solve problems."

"Well, that's a nice idea," said Ronnie.

Being patronized by a man twenty years his junior seemed a sure bet to be the highlight of the evening. Then Jennifer told Cora that she had grown up about half an hour from here and her mother still lived a few miles down the Parkway. "We're staying there tonight."

And that was the *real* reason for the dinner, he realized. To make the visit to Mom tax-deductible. Shanks was ready to slink home and pour himself something much stronger than you could find on the Big Bombay's wine list.

But even that pleasure had to be postponed. Jennifer had taken a liking to the quaint downtown area where the restaurant was located and wanted to take a stroll.

"What a beautiful old building!" she said as they passed a brick house. It had clearly been built as a residence, but now it contained one of the countless shops that sold pillows and placemats and other furnishings Shanks couldn't imagine anyone buying, except as gifts for people they didn't know well, or like much.

"It is nice, isn't it?" said Cora. "Shanks, what was here before this shop moved in?"

He closed his eyes and pictured it. "Masterpiece Videos."

"No," said Cora. "Masterpiece was on Second Street."

"They moved there from here. And before them, this was a camera store."

That was when Jennifer asked how long they had lived in the town and Shanks made his ill-considered reply.

"All I meant," he explained, "was that we've lived here so long that when I look at a store I usually see two or three that were there before."

"Like revised versions of a screenplay," Ronnie suggested.

"Or a palimpsest," said Jennifer.

Shanks' bushy eyebrows rose. "A palimpsest?"

"That's when a text is erased and another is written over it. Like on a scroll."

"I know what it is. I just—" He paused, looking for a way to end the sentence that didn't translate *I thought all actresses were dumb*.

She seemed amused. "I minored in classical studies. If you need any Latin translated, I'm your girl."

"Is that much help in Hollywood?"

"Less than you might hope. It got me a part as a slave in *Plato In Love*."

"We must have missed that one," said Cora.

"Trust me," said Jennifer, cheerfully. "Whatever you did instead was the two best-spent hours of the year. What did this insurance office used to be, Shanks?"

"A tax preparer."

"What about the curry place where we ate?" asked Ronnie.

"Guadalajara Grill. And before that, Naples Cuisine."

"I wondered why the decorations in the ladies room looked Mexican," said Jennifer. "I guess they didn't bother to repaint."

"Here's another entry for your memory banks," said Ronnie. "What do you think *this* one is going to be?"

A storefront had been blocked off by wooden boards, the windows covered with brown paper. They could hear banging and drilling inside.

"No idea," said Shanks

"They must be in a hurry to be working on Friday night. That's serious overtime."

"It used to be a card shop, but they went out of business a year ago. Actually that's only *half* a building. You see the jewelry store next door?"

Cora and Jennifer had already discovered the jewelers and were discussing the wares in the tiny window with what Shanks thought was far too much enthusiasm.

"I'm glad *they're* closed," Ronnie muttered.

"Amen. But there was an optician in there until last year. That space and the one under construction are really parts of the same building. You can't tell, because the façades are different. The whole place used to be a bookstore."

"Which chain?"

Shanks sighed. "This was back in the good old days. It was an independent shop. In fact, my first signing after we moved to town was right there."

"Ready to move on, ladies?" called Ronnie.

They stepped back from the window. "There's some great stuff in there," said Jennifer. "High-end bling."

"True," said Cora. "We need to come back when they're open. We can get some real jewelry bargains."

Shanks didn't believe that *jewelry* and *bargain* belonged in the same sentence, but he kept that thought to himself.

"Well, this evening has been a pleasure," said Ronnie, preparing his exit.

Shanks stopped. He looked back at the jewelry store and the empty shell next to it, reflecting on its glory days as Bremond's Books.

Then he started thinking fast.

"Are you coming, Shanks?" asked Cora. But Jennifer pointed to something in a dress shop window and they got distracted.

"Ronnie, I think you might be on to something."

The agent half-covered a yawn. "I wish I was on my way to bed. What do you mean?"

"You said how odd it was that they were doing construction on Friday night."

"Did I?"

"You did. Remember I told you those two stores used to be one? That jewelry store is brick on three sides, but I'll bet the landlord just put up a thin plaster wall between the two halves. Wouldn't you?"

"I suppose. What's your point?"

Shanks sighed. He had hoped the agent could figure it out with a little coaching. "If you wanted to break into that jewelry store, how would you do it?"

Ronnie frowned. "You couldn't. There's always people around and it would make too much noise—"

He stopped and stared at the construction site, with grinding and banging sounds still pouring out. "My God, Shanks. They're drilling into the jewelry store and making it look like they're just doing construction."

"You think so?"

"It's obvious." He fumbled for his cell phone. "I'm surprised you didn't figure it out yourself. I'm calling the cops."

"Good idea."

"I'll bet they even got the jeweler to turn off the alarms, because of the loud construction work."

Nice detail, Shanks thought approvingly.

"What's going on?" asked Cora.

"Let's all move down the block," said Shanks. "Ronnie just made an important discovery. We don't want to be too close to that store." He explained the theory.

Jennifer's eyes went wide. "Ronnie figured that out? Wow!"

Cora frowned at her husband. "Did he?"

He raised his eyebrows. "Who else?"

Ronnie closed the phone. "They're sending a car. This is incredible." He bit his lip. "Uh, what if we're wrong?"

Suddenly it's *we,* Shanks noted. "Then the cops were called over nothing. It wouldn't be the first time."

"This is so *cool,*" said Jennifer.

Cora laughed and squeezed Shanks' arm. "Way cool."

After the police rolled off the two couples went for ice cream at the Polar Parlor (previously Robot Donuts, previously Sweetums Candy, previously some other damned place.)

"That was *fantastic,*" bubbled Jennifer, waving her sorbet spoon.

"The looks on those jokers' faces when the cops marched them out in handcuffs," said Ronnie. "I'm glad I had my phone to take some pictures."

"We can blog it," said Jennifer.

"Do you really think it'll be in the paper, Shanks?"

"I don't see why not. You're gonna be a hero, Ronnie."

"A hero." The agent stopped with a spoonful of butter brickle halfway to his mouth.

"You know what?" said Cora, grinning at Shanks. "They ought to make a movie out of this."

He nodded gravely. "Too bad there's no market for mysteries."

"Who said that?" Ronnie demanded. "Mysteries are the next big thing. Shanks, do your books have capers like this?"

"Better ones, I hope."

"He said modestly," said Cora.

"Well, send me some," said Ronnie. "Let's see if we can wake up a studio or two."

"That would be great."

"I know some sharp guys, people who are always looking for new talent." Ronnie looked thoughtful. "New... How long ago was your first book published?"

"I forget," said Shanks.

We have lived in our town for more than two decades and it is absolutely true that I can look at a Chinese restaurant downtown and remember the wine store, the hippy organic place, the coffee shop, and the clothing store, that occupied the same space. I really liked the coffee shop. Oh, well.

It seemed like something Shanks could work with, and it fit a title I had had in my notebook for years. This is its first appearance in print.

Authors sometimes talk about a character rebelling against the part written for him or her. I have only experienced that twice and this story is one of them. After Jennifer says "This is so cool!" I expected Cora to say something typically skeptical. Instead she insisted on laughing and going along with the game. This showed me a side of her character I have tried to point out in some of the stories that follow.

Unfortunately, as you will see, in the next one I needed her to demonstrate her darker side.

~ Second Interlude ~

This appeared in my Wednesday spot at the Criminal Brief blog in 2010. It addresses a long-standing complaint of mine, as you can probably tell.

PROLOGUE FOR A SHANKS NOVEL
IN CASE I EVER WRITE ONE

PROLOGUE

He had hiked a mile into the woods and the gun was getting heavy.

She was walking ahead, much faster than him, as usual, almost running. Almost as if she sensed what was coming, but it was the way she always moved, full of energy, wanting to squeeze an extra minute into each hour, and cram twenty-five hours into every day.

It was the reason he had fallen in love with her. Ironic, now that he thought about it. He shifted the heavy bag from one shoulder to the other. Its burden was biting into him like a guilty conscience. A bird, something small and dark, flew across their path, calling loudly.

And now she was back, bouncing like a puppy. "Come on! I want to get to the top before sunset."

He thought about ending it right there. Just pull out the gun and put a stop to this terrible, agonizing prose.

Leopold Longshanks glared at his computer screen. He touched a macro button on the keyboard and sent the current file to an ever-growing folder called TRASH. He hated books with prologues. But his editor – who obviously didn't know anything or he would be a writer, not an editor – was insistent.

Shanks sighed. He tapped a key and tried again.

PROLOGUE

There is a rule in the publishing industry today that every mystery or suspense novel has to start with a murder. Preferably on the first page, but definitely in the first chapter. If the actual story doesn't happen to start with a life ending, the author is expected to create a prologue that features some satisfactory violent event, either yanked from later in the book, or dragged forward from some character's backstory.

This is cheap and stupid. It distorts the book and patronizes the reader.

This novel you are reading does not happen to begin with a murder. There will be deaths a-plenty but none that can be untimely ripped out of their proper niches and wedged into a prologue.

Here's a suggestion. I've been writing these books for a long time. Chances are you've read some of mine before and know the kind of books I write.

So let's have some faith in each other. You trust that I'll put in some high quality homicides when the time is right, and I'll trust that you'll read long enough to let the story develop.

We're grown-ups here. We can do this.

Ready? Begin.

SHANKS COMMENCES

"You write detective stories, don't you?" said the police officer.

Leopold Longshanks' usual reply to that question was "Guilty," but it seemed inappropriate tonight.

"That's right."

They were seated on the top floor of the college library, outside the Special Collections Room. Through its glass walls Shanks saw half a dozen cops at work. They seemed wildly out of place in the chamber, which looked like a Victorian gentleman's study with rugs, overstuffed chairs, and wood-paneled walls.

And lots and lots of bookcases.

There were two doors in the back wall. Shanks knew that one led to a climate-controlled vault for manuscripts. The other revealed the office of Dr. Ezra Rosetti, the director of Special Collections. That's where most of the police officers were going, because that's where the body had been found.

"Mr. Longshanks?" the cop repeated. His name was Lieutenant Steinbock.

"I'm sorry. I didn't hear you."

"I said I hope you aren't one of those writers who think you can help the police solve crimes."

"God forbid."

"I'm glad to hear that."

"I just make things up. I don't know anything about solving real crimes."

"Excellent." Steinbock opened his notebook.

"I do have one question, though." said Shanks. "Where are my books?"

"Excuse me?"

"I left a dozen of my novels sitting on the corner of that desk." He pointed through the glass. There was nothing on the big antique desk now except a phone and a blotter. "So who moved them?"

Steinbock frowned. He stood up and walked toward the door, muttering something under his breath. Shanks couldn't hear what he said, but he suspected it wasn't an expression of gratitude.

"What's missing exactly?"

"Twelve hardcover novels. All written by me."

He watched as Steinbock walked into the room and spoke to one of the uniformed cops.

Shanks sighed. It was going to be a long night.

The lieutenant resumed his seat. "We'll look for your books. Now, you'd better start at the beginning."

"Really?"

"What does that mean?"

"The current wisdom in writing fiction is to start in the middle, where things get interesting, and then go back to fill in whatever seems necessary."

The detective seemed to be at a loss for words, but his glare spoke volumes.

"Never mind," said Shanks. "The beginning it is. Two years ago I received a letter from Calvin Floyd."

"The librarian."

"Director of the college library, yes. One of my novels won an award, and he sent congratulations on behalf of my alma mater. We exchanged quite a few emails and eventually he called to talk about my future plans."

"What do you mean, I'm without a shoe?" Shanks had asked. He looked down to his office carpet where a rather nice pair of brown loafers covered his argyles.

"I said you were without *issue*," said Floyd, over the phone.

"Oh, I've got plenty of issues."

Floyd sighed. His voice was high-pitched but pleasant. "Now, you're teasing me. I mean you and your wife have no children, so I'm wondering if you have decided where you will leave your manuscripts and other papers. Future generations of readers and scholars will want to study them."

That was a shock. Shanks had more or less assumed that he and Cora would live beyond the end of literacy, which might be next Tuesday the way things seemed to be going.

To his surprise, Cora had thought it was a fine idea. "If the college wants to cart some of your papers out of here when you're gone, that's some junk I won't have to deal with."

"Maybe I could arrange for them to cart *me* off, as well."

"Now, that would be a full-service institution. Seriously, Shanks, this is a chance to be honored now and honored later, too. You've earned it. What's the downside?"

Well, the obvious one was that it would allow his literary remains to be poked with a stick by any future grad student with time on his hands and a desire to prove Leopold Longshanks' work had been inspired by oedipal issues, alcoholism, or fear of crabgrass.

On the other hand, it might be fun to plant a few jokers in the deck. For example, he could fake some evidence that his recent noir extravaganza, *Bloodsoaked,* had been inspired by the novels of Charlotte Bronte. Let future professors ponder *that* one.

"So that's why you're here?" asked Lieutenant Steinbock. "To deliver your papers?"

"Well, most of them won't come until after I die. But we signed the formal agreement last fall and the college invited me to be the commencement speaker. The dozen novels were sort of a down payment."

"And when exactly did Mr. Floyd tell you who would actually control your papers?"

"You mean the head of Special Collections," Shanks said, casting a glance at the cops in the glass room. "Not until I got to campus this morning."

"So you didn't know your old enemy would be in charge of your legacy?"

"Wow," said Shanks, raising a bushy eyebrow. "I'm trying to figure out how many things are wrong with that sentence. My legacy, as you call it, lies in my published works. My rough drafts and grocery lists are only interesting, if at all, because of the actual books. And anyway, Dr. Rosetti wasn't my enemy."

"What would you call him?"

"A former professor. The worst thing he ever did was give me a D."

"In Creative Writing, I understand. That must have hurt for a future writer."

"Actually, when I took his course I was hoping to be a trumpet player. But let's assume I was outraged. Wouldn't you say that making a living as an author all these years was revenge enough? I hardly needed to— May I ask how he was killed?"

"Letter opener to the throat, Mr. Longshanks. How did you feel when you found out he was going to be in charge of your papers?"

"Astonished, mostly. I graduated about thirty years ago. I had assumed that most of my old professors had gone to their rewards by now, or at least to Florida."

"Dr. Rosetti says the snowy winters here are good for him," Calvin Floyd had explained. Shanks and Cora were in the library director's office, having just had a tour of the campus. The librarian looked a bit grim as he told them this, as if it were regrettable news.

Shanks thought about what it must be like to be Rosetti's boss. He shuddered.

"I'm surprised he's working in here. He's not a librarian, is he?"

"Oh my, no." Floyd spoke with uncharacteristic force. He was a thin man, and could seem a little vague until he started talking about books. Or, as it turned out, Rosetti. "His doctorate is in English. But he's been a collector of rare books for most of his life, and…."

"He donated them to the college," Cora guessed.

"Some of them."

With strings attached, Shanks thought. *Rosetti controls Special Collections or they don't get more of his treasures.* You almost had to admire the old scoundrel.

"Welcome, Mr. Longshanks!" The newcomer was a bright-eyed

young woman. "What a pleasure to meet you at last. I heard you speak at a mystery convention a few years ago. I'm Dina Lundin."

"Mr. Floyd mentioned you," Shanks said. "You teach a course on mysteries, don't you?"

"When my boss lets me." She stepped aside and Shanks realized a man had been standing behind her. The department head was almost as short and round as one of Santa's elves, and even had a gray beard.

"Richard Upton. It's a pleasure."

They four of them shook hands. "Well, thanks for letting Dina teach mysteries."

'There's a price," she said, cheerfully. "I have to do two sections of freshman comp for every fun course."

"Then I truly appreciate your sacrifice," said Shanks.

"Dina's great with the frosh," said Upton. "Personally, I can't stand the little monsters."

Floyd had been talking on the phone. Now he hung up with the look of a man trying to conceal annoyance. "Excuse me, everyone. President Warren has taken our other guests directly to the Special Collections Room, so we had better join them."

Floyd marched out into the main floor of the library and the rest of the group followed. An assistant hurried up to the director and they talked together as they walked.

Shanks heard the two professors talking behind him. "Think it was an accident?" asked Upton.

"Nope," said Lundin.

"What do you mean?" asked Cora.

Upton laughed. "Our president gravitates toward power. When she escorts wealthy donors to the library it never occurred to her to bring them to Cal."

"You mean Rosetti runs the library?" asked Shanks.

"No. He has no desire to. He just wants to run Special Collections as his own personal kingdom and since that's the part alumni and donors care about—"

"It's all the president cares about," Cora finished. "Sounds like the tail wagging the dog."

"I bought a bottle of rare champagne years ago," Upton said. "I was saving it for my fiftieth wedding anniversary. The day Ezra Rosetti retired from my department I popped the cork."

"Didn't that annoy your wife?"

"It was her idea. She said my not being Rossetti's boss would add years to our marriage."

Floyd was waiting for them beside the elevator. "Lots of preparations for tonight's dinner," he said apologetically.

Why is the librarian in charge of the dinner, Shanks wondered. Maybe they needed some cookbooks.

"So you came up here," said Lieutenant Steinbock. He wasn't drumming his fingers on the table, but looked like he might start at any moment.

"Correct," said Shanks. "President Warren was already in the Special Collections Room with the other two guests."

The cop looked at his notes. "That would be Mrs. Velma Preese and Mr. Grey G. Johnson, the other speakers."

"They aren't making speeches. They're just getting honorary degrees."

"Yeah? In what?"

"It doesn't matter much. Honorary degrees are for achievement, not for knowing anything."

"So what did they achieve, exactly?"

"As I understand it, money."

Velma Preese was a gray-haired, confused-looking woman in her sixties. Upton had explained that her husband was an alumnus of the college who had left the school a lot of rare books in his will.

"Walter hardly ever *mentioned* this place," she had explained. "He just complained about the dunning letters they sent every year."

President Janice Warren – a bright-eyed politician in her early fifties – tried to hide her amusement. "I don't think our Development Office would be happy to hear the alumni newsletter described in quite that way. I must remember to tell them."

Grey G. Johnson was a wealthy alum in his sixties who had decided to make his gift while he was still alive and kicking. He was paying for a new gym.

"Why is it always a gym?" Cora had muttered. "Do all rich men have fond memories of playing football?"

"More likely," said Shanks, "they have grim memories of being pushed around by football players."

"Never spent much time in the library," Johnson was saying. He was tall and distinguished-looking, with a smug air. "The business courses didn't require much more reading than the textbooks, thank God. I'm not much of a bookworm."

"And how have you make your money?" Cora asked.

"In money, mostly. I finance start-up companies. It's gambling, but better odds then the casinos."

"So we're honoring three businessmen this year," said a new voice.

It sent a chill down Shanks' spine. Dr. Ezra Rosetti had appeared from his private office

He looked, as Cora put it later, like a grumpy Albert Einstein: wild gray hair, a sweater with elbow patches, and a perpetual scowl.

Shanks realized with a shock that, except for the graying hair, the man hadn't changed a bit. It must be true that some people don't get wrinkles, they give them.

"How did Professor Rosetti get along with everyone?" Steinbock asked.

"Let's see," said Shanks. "He fawned over Mrs. Preese, talking about what a wonderful gift her husband had made to the collection." Not to the library, or the college, Shanks had noted. "Apparently the books were early American literature and quite valuable. He was excited about them."

"How did he feel about your contribution?"

Shanks paused. "I'm trying to decide between *scorn* and *contempt*."

"The famous Mr. Longshanks," Rosetti had said, or more accurately, sneered. "Have you learned the difference between preterit and past perfect?"

"I practice constantly." *What would annoy you most? Probably if I look amused.* Shanks smiled.

"That's right," said Upton. "You took a course from Dr. Rosetti, didn't you?"

"Creative Writing," said Shanks. "He gave me a D."

President Warren laughed. "Isn't it nice when a student turns out better than we expect?"

"It must be," said Rosetti.

"What do you mean about three businessmen?" asked Cora.

"I mean your husband doesn't write *literature*. He's turning out a product for the masses, so he's a businessman, just like Mr. Johnson there, except Mr. Johnson doesn't claim to be a creative artist."

The wealthy alum smiled. "Some people think my annual reports are a bit *too* creative."

"Please, Ezra," said Warren. "Don't insult our guests."

"It's not an insult to be told I write for popular taste," said Shanks. "Puts me in the same category as Dickens or Twain. Who was the most popular author in Shakespeare's day?"

"Shakespeare," said Upton, grinning right through his beard.

Rosetti's face, on the other hand, was stony. "So that's who you compare yourself to?"

"Of course not. I'm nowhere *near* as popular as those gentlemen were. But I aspire to be. And speaking of aspiration, here is the first phase of my contribution to your collection." He handed over the hefty pile of first editions of his novels. Rosetti placed them on a corner of his desk without a glance, and rubbed his hand on his corduroy jacket.

He actually wiped his hand, Shanks thought, amazed. *In case he caught any cooties from my books.*

But worse was on the way. "I read one of your little books in preparation for this meeting." Shanks guessed what was coming next. Rosetti named a novel that had received a stunningly negative review in a national magazine the year before. "I'm afraid I didn't think it was as good as the critics claimed."

Since punching the old coot was not an option Shanks smiled more broadly. "Well, now you have some more to try."

"And Shanks has promised us his papers," said Dina Lundin. "We will be the center for Longshanks studies!"

"I'm sure that will keep us hopping, my dear," said Rosetti. "Fortunately there's plenty of room in the College History section of the vault."

Dina frowned. "You make it sound like you're going to lock his papers up in maximum security so that no one can get hurt by them."

Rosetti gave her a lemony smile. "I'm afraid I don't know as much about prisons as you. I don't read that kind of book."

"Why is everyone so *cranky?*" asked Mrs. Preese.

"Just artistic differences," said Professor Upton, pleasantly. "Let's take a look at these books your husband so generously donated."

Grey G. Johnson shook his head in amusement. "I take it the professor here thinks you're a short-term investment, Shanks."

At least he wasn't being compared to a junk bond. "Come again?"

"Your books are popular now, but the doctor is interested in writers whose value will increase in time."

Rosetti looked even more irritated. "Not everything is about money."

"No? Hey, Janice." President Warren looked up instantly. "The doc says my money isn't important."

"It's important to *us,*" she said firmly. "Cal, is it time for dinner?"

"Where are we going for dinner?" Cora asked. 'That wasn't clear on the invitation."

"Just down the hall," said Calvin Floyd. "In fact, it *is* time to go."

"Eating in the library?" asked Shanks. "I seem to recall getting demerits for that."

"You *rogue,*" said Cora.

"So he led you all to the big room," said Steinbock.

"The Great Hall, yes."

"Did you all leave Special Collections together?"

Shanks closed his eyes, picturing it. "Yes."

"And who was the last one out?"

"Rosetti. But we arrived more or less as a group."

"Now, this is *something*," said Cora, with satisfaction.

The Great Hall looked just like a college library should, with twenty foot ceilings and picture windows above the wooden bookcases that lined the walls.

"Recently restored through a generous gift by alumni," said Calvin Floyd. Rosetti wasn't the only one who could brag about bringing in the bucks.

The long tilted desks Shanks remembered had been removed for the dinner and most of the room was filled with long tables covered with white cloths. College students in dark jackets stood by, ready to wait on the tables.

"So you went to your table," the Lieutenant prompted.

"No. We were a little early. President Warren had to huddle with the board of trustees over some budget emergency and suggested we look at the art for a while."

At one end of the hall someone had placed a dozen free-standing walls, the kind that make up office cubicles, and they were covered with paintings, drawings and photos by this year's graduating art majors.

"And how long was it before you were called to dinner?"

"About twenty minutes, I think."

"Did you see any of the group from Special Collections during that time?"

"Two of them."

"What do you think you're doing, Shanks?" Cora had asked.

"Just admiring the art, dear." Shanks sipped wine.

"I can see that. You've been stuck in front of the nudes for about ten minutes."

"Is that what they are? A bit abstract for my taste."

"Not *that* abstract. Come over here. There's a very—"

"Has anyone seen my keys?" Dr. Rosetti had rushed up, eyes wide. "The keys to Special Collections. I put them in my pants pocket after I locked the door."

"No, you didn't," said Shanks. "You put them in your *coat* pocket."

Rosetti frowned. "I never do that."

"You did today. Go check your coat."

The old man hurried off without a word.

"What a charmer," said Cora.

"Always was. Now, where were we?"

"About to look at some landscapes."

"Oh. Right."

"So Dr. Rosetti went out to the hall where the coat racks had been placed," said Steinbock.

"Presumably. I never saw him again. A few minutes later one of the servers called everyone to sit down. The whole gang we'd met in Special Collections ate together – except the president, who dined on the platform with the trustees. Rosetti never arrived." Shanks eyebrows dropped in a frown. "Why all this interest in our group, by the way?"

The cop ignored his question. "Who was the last person to get to the table?"

"Mr. Johnson and Professor Lundin came up together. They were discussing the art."

"Did anyone leave the table during dinner?"

"I don't believe so. Not until President Warren got up to speak. Then Cal Floyd said he was going to look for Rosetti. He'd been fretting about the old man's absence."

At the time Shanks had wondered whether the library director was simply looking for an excuse to avoid the President's speech. Actually she wasn't bad at all, although she had thanked the crowd for their "generous and fulsome applause." Did she know what fulsome *meant?*

When the president had finished to polite applause a tall man in a gray suit had stepped to the lectern, introduced himself as Lieutenant Steinbock and announced that he had some bad news.

The evening careened downhill from there.

"Lieutenant?" A young cop was standing in the doorway of the Special Collections Room. Steinbock walked over for a brief consultation. He came back with a satisfied smile.

'We've solved the mystery of your missing books, Mr. Longshanks." He said the word *mystery* as someone else might have said *fairy tale.*

"Terrific. Where are they?"

"Apparently Dr. Rosetti put them on a cart to send to be cataloged."

Shanks peered through the glass and saw two book trucks not far from the desk. "Interesting. He must have done that after he came back, because they were definitely on the desk when we left. So he had a little time in there before he died."

"Thanks for pointing that out," said Steinbock, not sounding grateful.

Shanks didn't waste time wondering what the cop was so sour about. He was thinking about the two carts. "I see there are labels on the carts. May I ask what they say?"

Steinbock had better eyes. "Your books are on the cart that says CATALOG FOR THE LITERATURE COLLECTION. The other one says CATALOG FOR THE COLLEGE HISTORY COLLECTION."

Shanks frowned. "That's wrong."

"Read them for yourself."

"No, I mean Rosetti would never put my books on the literature cart."

The lieutenant heaved a deep sigh. "I'm only a humble police officer, Mr. Longshanks, but aren't novels considered literature?"

"Yes and no. I mean, they are, but Rosetti thought mysteries shouldn't be. He called them genre fiction, or sub-literature."

"But he accepted the books for the collection."

"Because I'm an alumnus of the college. You see? If Rosetti put the books anywhere it would have been on the College History cart."

Steinbock was stone-faced. "Are you saying someone killed Dr. Rosetti in order to sneak your books into the literature collection?"

"Of course not. I have a few eccentric fans but none that are totally insane." He hoped he sounded confident about that.

"Then why would the murderer take the books off the desk and put them on that cart?"

Good question. Shanks gazed through the glass wall, trying to picture the scene.

*You steal the keys from Rosetti's coat. You come to the locked room
to do – what? Whatever you have in mind, Rosetti catches you and you
kill him. Then – or perhaps before? – you grab the books off the edge of
the desk, and you stick them on the literature cart.*

Why?

To clear a spot on the desk? No.

To conceal them? No.

Ah.

"To fill a hole."

"Excuse me?"

"The killer removed something from the literature cart. That left a
hole and he used the first books he saw to fill it."

Steinbock frowned "What books did he remove?"

"I have no idea. But come to think of it, Mrs. Preese brought those
valuable books her husband had donated."

The cop nodded and stood up. "Zeman! Go get the library director,
Floyd. See if he has a list of the books that were donated today."

"I was wondering," said Shanks. "Could I have a look at my books?"

"What for?"

"I saw them not long before the killer handled them. Maybe he left
something I might notice."

Steinbock shook his head. "No thanks, Mr. Longshanks. We don t
need any amateurs messing up our crime scene tonight."

"I wasn't trying to—"

"You just mind your own business, and let us—"

"Excuse me," said a very cold voice.

Calvin Floyd had arrived, accompanied by President Warren, who
did not look happy.

"Detective," she said, in a tone that made even Shanks sit a little
straighter, "may I ask why you are *screaming* at our guest of honor?"

Steinbock stood up. "I just want to make sure he knows why he's
here. And why he's *not.*"

"I'm sure Mr. Longshanks understands his duties perfectly," said the president. "Unlike some people."

"Excuse me," said Shanks. "There's really no need for—"

"It's late," said the president. "I'm sending our guests home. Unless you plan to jail us all for the night?"

The cop's face said he was seriously considering it. Then he shrugged. "Zeman, do we have prints from every person of interest?"

"All except Dr. Lundin," said the young cop. "She says it's a violation of her civil rights."

Shanks made a face. Why did it have to be his fan causing trouble?

"Dina is the head of the Human Rights Task Force on campus," said Floyd, somewhat apologetically.

Cora had arrived. "I've never been fingerprinted before. It's not as messy as I thought."

"We're all leaving," said President Warren. "Now." She glared at the cop, daring him to disagree.

Steinbock nodded. "Thanks for your cooperation."

Shanks dawdled on the way out and landed himself beside the cop. "Lieutenant, Dina Lundin was the only person at our table who drank soda. If they haven't cleared the table yet you can get finger—"

"Thank you *very much*," said Steinbock, loud enough for everyone to hear. "We don't need any more of your help."

As they waited for the car that would drive them back to the motel Cora asked: "What's the problem with that sourpuss cop? How did you make him so mad at you?"

"I swear, he was mad at me when we met. I never had a chance to annoy him."

"Huh. Why?"

"Beats me. Maybe a mystery writer bit him when he was a child."

Between being a murder suspect and having to give a commencement speech Shanks figured he wouldn't get much sleep, but he conked out as soon as he hit the pillow. At dawn he was wide awake.

He showered and dressed without his wife and sat down at the table to review his speech. He had twenty minutes to pass on all the wisdom he had acquired over the years. Cora, his beloved helpmate, had asked how he would fill the last nineteen minutes. Shanks looked at his opening jokes with a critical eye. Perhaps they were inappropriate the day after a professor got murdered. Even Rosetti.

He copied the speech to a new file on his laptop and began tinkering with the opening. Someone knocked at the door.

It was Lieutenant Steinbock. *Probably come to warn me again about playing detective.*

"Good morning, Mr. Longshanks. I saw your light was on."

"Morning, Lieutenant."

"Can I buy you a cup of coffee? The place downstairs is open."

Surprise, surprise. "I'll leave a note for my wife."

The coffee shop was refreshingly small-town. No macchiato or cappuccinos, just regular or decaf, and the waitress left the carafe.

Shanks poured two sugars into his cup and waited for the cop to stop staring into his own black brew.

Steinbock finally spoke, with obvious reluctance. "Mr. Longshanks, I need to apologize for my behavior."

Shanks frowned. "You do?"

"I was out of line last night. I was rude and—"

"You were just doing your job."

A ferocious scowl. "Would you let me get through this, please?"

Shanks blinked. "Oh. You said you *need* to apologize, not that you want to. President Warren ordered you to."

"The college president does not tell me what to do."

"I didn't mean to imply—"

"She spoke to the mayor, who spoke to the police chief. *He* tells me what to do."

"I'm sorry," said Shanks. "And I'm surprised too. When I was in college we had the impression that a police officer who annoyed the college president was likely to get a hardy handshake and possibly a promotion."

Steinbock nodded. "The town-gown rivalry. There was still a bit of that around when I started. But it ended nine years ago."

"Really? What happened?"

"The wire plant closed."

"And suddenly the college was the biggest employer in town."

"Yeah, but that wasn't the main thing. Some of the smart guys at the school applied for a huge grant to use the factory complex as a kind of laboratory." He gazed at the ceiling, looking for a phrase he had obviously memorized. "Studying Nature's Reclamation of a Post-Industrial Landscape. The grant has been renewed every year and students take field trips there to study the decay of the buildings. Ecology students, engineers, artists."

"My word."

"Every fall scientists come from around the country for a conference about researching old factories. Every spring professors come from around the country to learn how to do the same thing in their own towns."

Shanks' eyebrows rose. "In other words, the college turned a derelict plant into a money-spinner for the city."

Steinbock nodded. "And that means that if President Warren told the mayor to come over and paint her house, all he'd say was 'what color?' Getting a cop chewed out was easy-peasey."

"Well, I'm sorry that happened. You have my word that she'll hear you and I are best buddies now."

Steinbock shuddered. "I'd appreciate that."

Shanks poured them both more coffee. "I asked you last night: why are you concentrating on the group that was in Special Collections? Couldn't it have been anyone who came to the library for the dinner?"

The cop's face twitched as he struggled with the instinct to tell the civilian to butt out. Shanks had to hide a smile behind his coffee cup.

Politics won. "You noticed the napkins with the presidential crests that were on your table?"

Shanks nodded.

"The killer used one to wipe the letter opener. Granted someone else could have swiped one off the table, but the most likely explanation—"

"The killer was probably someone who had dropped by our table to put their stuff down before they went to look at the art. Just like my wife and I did. Were any napkins missing?"

"There were extras on the table. Of course there were the same napkins on the high table too, but the servers swear no one went near it until the board members came in together. The biggest news is that we found the missing books. As you suggested, they were the ones Mrs. Preese brought."

"That's great. Where were they?"

"Not far from the Special Collections Room, tucked behind the books on the top shelf of one of the book cases. I understand they call them *stacks*. They were behind books on the ancient Hittites, if that means anything."

"Not to me." Shanks decided to press his luck. "Any fingerprints?"

"Yes, but there weren't any on *your* books. Someone wiped them clean."

"Now, that's interesting." Shanks closed his eyes. "The culprit stole Rosetti's keys. He snuck down the hall to the Special Collections Room and swiped the rare books and hid them in the book stacks outside. But he realized he had left a hole on the cart. He went back to fill the hole with my books. That's when Rosetti caught him. After disposing of the professor the thief was careful to remove the fingerprints."

Shanks scowled. "Why didn't he wipe the rare books? Because they were already hidden and he wanted to get back to the dinner party before someone came looking for Rosetti."

He opened his eyes and saw Steinbock staring at him with interest. "Is that how you write? Seeing the scene the way it happened?"

"On good days. Sometimes I just pile words together like bricks and hope nothing falls off."

Steinbock looked thoughtful. "Okay. Now tell me whose fingerprints were on the stolen books."

Shanks sipped coffee. "Mrs. Preese, of course, because she brought them. Rosetti, because he accepted them from her. I have no idea who else."

That seemed to please the lieutenant. *Maybe he was afraid I was using magical powers.*

"Calvin Floyd and Richard Upton."

"The library director and the head of the English Department. So they, along with Mrs. Preese, are your suspects."

"The major suspects, yes." Steinbock smiled. "And I can tell you that my best interrogators are sitting down separately with each of them right now. We'll go over their stories until we find out what actually happened. This is how crimes are *really* solved, Mr. Longshanks. Not hunches. Not intuition. Just solid, one-step-at-a-time police work. You wouldn't – What are you staring at?"

"Sorry. I was just waiting for a chance to tell you that Velma Preese is the killer."

Steinbock threw his notebook down on the table. "You can't possibly know that. How can you even *claim* to know that?"

"Process of elimination. It wasn't Floyd because he was the library director."

The lieutenant scowled. "And they never commit murder?"

"They might, from time to time. But they have keys to their own buildings. Why risk drawing Rosetti's attention by stealing his keys?"

"Maybe so he wouldn't be the obvious suspect."

"All he would have had to do was leave the door unlocked when he left. Everyone would assume Rosetti had failed to lock the door. I saw Rosetti turn the key, but I couldn't swear he did it correctly. That would have even given Floyd a reason to fire him, which he would have loved."

Steinbock thought that one over for the length of a sip of coffee. "Okay. What about the department head?"

"Upton's barely five feet tall. Why would he hide the books on the top shelf? Even using a kickstand or a chair he couldn't have been sure he'd gotten the books out of the sight of a taller person. Not to mention the difficulty he would have had getting them out later."

"But the Preese woman was donating the books. Why steal them?"

"Now how could I know that? On the other hand—"

Steinbock sighed.

"The books were really a gift from her late husband, not her. Maybe she didn't know what they were worth, until Rosetti started talking about them that day. Then she had a couple of glasses of wine before the dinner party and started thinking it was more than the college deserved."

"Huh," said the cop.

"It seemed like a spur-of-the-moment crime, didn't it?"

The cop opened his phone and hit speed dial. "Zeman? It's me. Who's interrogating the Preese woman? Good. Tell 'em to ask her about her financials, and how much the books were worth. Yeah, she's probably it. Get back to me."

He shut the phone. "Damn it."

"What is it?"

"Preese is another guest of the college. President Warren's going to have my head on a platter."

Shanks shook his head. "Warren's a complete professional. Once she sees how the wind is blowing she'll talk about the late Mr. Preese and forget his widow exists. But warn her before commencement, if you can. That way she'll owe you one."

"Good idea. Uh… I guess ought to thank you again."

He hadn't thanked Shanks once, but who was counting? "Think nothing of it."

Steinbock pushed his coffee cup around the table. "This will probably end with a press conference."

"I'd be grateful if you kept my name out of it."

"Really?" The cop was astonished. "I thought writers loved publicity."

"Oh, we do. If you want to tell the reporters that my latest book is an unforgettable page-turner, I'm all for it. But a mystery writer helping to solving a crime?" He shook his head. "That's a parlor trick. A talking dog. It would be like *you* becoming famous for writing novels."

"Uff," said Steinbock. He changed color so dramatically that Shanks thought he might be choking. The man was actually *blushing*.

And then Shanks understood it all. The hostility. The sneers.

"Lieutenant," he said, "are you by any chance a writer?"

"Trying to be." Steinbock suddenly found his coffee cup fascinating. "Halfway through a novel. Been halfway for almost a year."

"I know that feeling. Is it a mystery?"

"God, no. No offense, Mr. Longshanks, but that stuff is junk."

Shanks sighed. "Too bad you never met Dr. Rosetti You two would have really hit it off."

"Since you asked," Steinbock said in a rush, "my book is about a teenage boy who was supposed to be the first in his family to go to college, but his father gets injured in a car accident and there's this girl—"

Shanks, who hadn't asked, nodded. "A coming of age novel."

The cop looked sick. "You mean there are so many books like mine that they *have a name for it?*"

"There's always room for another good one."

"Can you tell me the names of some of the good ones?"

"Hand me your notebook."

"They released you," said Cora. She was applying make-up. "I was ready to start calling bail bondsmen."

"There isn't a jail in this town that can hold me. That's a lovely dress." He went out on a limb. "Is it new?"

"It is." She spun around to show off the light blue print. "I bought it to celebrate your commencement speech. And because I didn't have anything appropriate for sitting around outside on a hot June day. *You* have to wear a long black dress the whole time."

Shanks frowned. "I'd forgotten about the academic gown. And a mortarboard, *plus* the hood for the honorary degree. I'll melt."

"That's the price of fame, I guess. What did the fuzz want?"

"Oh. Turns out Steinbock is a would-be novelist. He asked for some advice."

"I hope he didn't want you to read his manuscript."

Shanks shook his head. "He didn't think it was my style. When is the car supposed to pick us up for the president's breakfast?"

"In about ten minutes. That reminds me. Janice Warren called. She asked if you could work a mention of Dr. Rosetti into your speech."

"Please tell me you said no."

"I said you would be glad to."

"That's going to change the whole tone of the thing." He slumped into a chair. "Besides, it means I'll have to say something *nice* about the man. How can I do that?

"No problem, darling." She kissed him on his bald spot. "You write fiction for a living."

You might possibly have noticed that the three stories previous to "Shanks Commences" were all rejected. If you don't think that sort of thing makes a writer nervous, you are crazy. So it felt great when this story was not only accepted, but made the cover of the May 2012 issue of HITCHCOCK'S.

This story has more links to reality than most of them. First of all, most of the characters share a name with the bloggers at Criminal Brief: James Lincoln Warren, Melodie Johnson Howe, Leigh Lundin, Steve Steinbock, John M. Floyd, and Deborah Upton. Velma was the name of our flirty secretary, a throwback to thirties private eye fiction, invented by Leigh.

Calvin Floyd slightly resembles Bob Sabin who was my boss and advisor when I was an undergrad working in the Beeghly Library at Juniata College. The Special Collections Room somewhat resembles the room at William Paterson College (now University) in Wayne, New Jersey, when I worked there in the 1980s. And the Great Hall is reminiscent of the Main Reading Room at Western Washington University. Students call it the Harry Potter Room because of a similarity to the dining hall at Hogwarts.

Dr. Rosetti, I am delighted to say, is entirely imaginary.

SHANKS' RIDE

"I don't think my alcohol level is over the legal limit," said Leopold Longshanks. "I could probably drive home all right. But I figure there's no point in taking chances."

"I know," said the taxi driver. "You've told me that three times."

"Oh." Shanks considered. "Then maybe I *do* need a ride."

"Hop in."

Ed, Ross, and Martin had popped out of the bar, none too steadily, and they waved enthusiastically as the cab pulled away from the curb.

"Did I give you my address?"

"Twice. Looks like you guys had quite a party."

"Celebrating." Shanks wormed his way down into a comfortable corner of the back seat. "One of my friends just reached the bestseller list for the first time."

The driver glanced in his rear view mirror. He was perhaps thirty, with long black hair tied in a ponytail. "Your friend a writer?"

"Yep. Me too. In fact everyone at the party was an author – at least everyone who stayed this late."

"So you write books. Have I ever heard of you?"

Shanks sighed. "Oh, absolutely. Unquestionably."

"How could you possibly know that?"

"If I couldn't know, then why did you ask?"

"Great. A wiseguy drunk."

"I'm not *a* drunk," said Shanks. "I'm a mystery writer who happens to *be* drunk."

A drunk. *B* drunk. What came next? *C D drunk? Yes, we C D drunk.*

He had definitely been overserved, as the phrase went. What would Cora say?

Well, he knew the answer to that. His wife wouldn't say anything when he arrived because she would have been asleep for hours. When they woke in the morning – him with his hangover and Cora with her annoying cheerfulness – he would tell her that they would have to go back to the bar to get his Toyota.

His wife would think for a moment. Then she would sigh and say "I'm glad you didn't try to drive." Because she knew that complaining about his drinking would make him less likely to call a cab next time.

If Cora ever complained about the taxi – in effect, saying that getting home sober was more important than getting home safely – it would meant that she had decided he *was* a drunk. At that point, Shanks knew, he would have to give up his semi-annual booze-ups.

"You say you write mysteries," said the driver – Tom Beal, according to his posted license. "Does that mean you know how to solve crimes?"

"No," said Shanks. "No, no, no, no. The police solve crimes. I just make stuff up."

"On TV writers are *always* solving crimes."

"On TV," said Shanks. "People can fly. Co-workers have affairs and keep working together. And people always tell the truth under torture."

"Okay, okay. I get it."

Silence reigned for a while and Shanks was drifting toward sleep when Beal said: "Listen, just to pass the time—"

"No."

"No, what?"

"You want to tell me about your old Aunt Hortense getting murdered and how the police don't know who the killer was. I'll save us both some trouble. I don't know either."

"You're a real smart mouth," Beal complained. "I don't *have* an Aunt Hortense. And I never knew anyone who got murdered."

"Lucky for you."

More silence. Then: "But there was a theft once. I had three friends and one of them stole something. I wake up nights thinking about it."

Shanks sighed. "Okay, I surrender. What did they steal from you?"

"From me? Nothing. Well, my job, I guess. Best job I ever had."

"And what was that?"

"I used to be a roadie for Zinc Heart."

"That was a rock band, I presume?"

Tom Beal stole another look in the mirror, eyes narrowed. "How *old* are you?"

"Twenty years your senior, more or less. That means the last new band I got excited about just entered the Rock and Roll Hall of Fame."

"You have to be in the business twenty-five years for that."

"Exactly. But I take it Tin Heart—"

"Zinc Heart!"

"Sorry. They were something special?"

"Hell, yes. They were the best thing to ever hit Industrial-Goth. Their first CD…"

Shanks let the rest of the sermon flow over him without attempting to catch any of it. When Beal slowed down he asked: "And what did they have to do with you?"

"I was one of their roadies, man. I was *with the band.* Traveled in their bus. Heard every song from backstage. You know how many people would kill for that?"

"Too many. What exactly does a roadie do?"

"Depends. Zinc Heart usually had four. Steve kept the axes in tune. That's guitars."

"Even I knew that. Go on."

"Pepe was the drum wrangler. K.C. ran wardrobe and make-up. I was speakers, mics and cables. And one of those three shafted me, man."

"How so?"

"We were playing the Passaic Theatre. Smaller than most of the gigs we did that year, but the band came from Wayne, and the first important show they did was at the Passaic."

"So it was a sentimental favorite," Shanks said.

"Bingo. But two hours before the show Rats came out of his dressing room screaming his head off."

"Who was Rats?"

More eye-rolling. "I keep forgetting you're a musical illiterate. Rats Maddox. He was the lead singer. Wrote most of their lyrics, too."

"Got it. What was he mad about?"

"Somebody stole his blow, man."

"Blow? You mean cocaine?"

"No, soap bubbles. Of *course* I mean coke. Rats used to spend half his royalties on nose candy."

"I'm sorry to hear that. Where did he keep it?"

"Some fan gave him a little metal statue of a soldier. Looked like the band's logo."

"Are you sure he hadn't misplaced it? Or discarded it out of paranoia?"

"I know he didn't and I'll tell you why in a minute. But you have to understand, Rats was *nuts*. I mean freaking wild. This is how crazy he was: he wanted to *call the police.*"

Shanks couldn't help grinning. "He was going to ask the cops to find his illegal drugs for him?" A description of Lord Byron popped into his head: *mad, bad, and dangerous to know.*

Uh oh. He only quoted people when he was drunk.

"Like I said, nuts. Seamus talked him out of it. Seamus Bolland, lead guitarist. You've never heard of him either."

"Right again."

"By then it was time for the show. So Rats made a big announcement. If his stolen property was returned to his dressing room it would be don't ask, don't tell."

"I think you mean, no questions asked."

"Whatever. So they did the gig. And it stank, cause Rats was too mad to function."

"Or maybe too straight," Shanks offered.

"Could be."

"And did the dope magically reappear?"

"Yup. Somebody opened his dressing room and threw the soldier on the floor. Lucky thing it didn't bust or there would have been a really crazy clean-up party."

"I can imagine. Was any missing?"

"Rats didn't think so. But now he was *really* mad. Until then he wasn't sure it was one of his crew that swiped it. But he figured it had to be someone who heard his speech, so he was determined to find out who."

"What happened to no questions asked?"

"Turns out he lied about that. Besides, he had a clue."

'What was that?"

"The soldier's sash was a piece of red ribbon, and it had torn off. Maybe the size of a Band-Aid, but bright red. Rats figured maybe the thief hadn't noticed it."

Shanks tried to picture a cocaine thief wearing a red Band-Aid. He had a feeling he was losing track of the story.

"So Rats had all the crew empty their pockets. Didn't find anything."

"Did that settle it?"

"You don't know Rats. He had everybody hunting all over the damn theatre in pairs, so that the bad guy couldn't hide the evidence. Then he marched the roadies onto the tour bus where we all had lockers. We opened them and I'll be damned if that scrap of red ribbon wasn't in my locker. I thought he was gonna kill me."

"But he didn't," said Shanks.

"No. Steve and Pepe got between us. But he canned me on the spot. My dream job, gone."

"A shame. Tell me more about the set-up. Rats had his own dressing room? Was it locked?"

"Locked, yeah, but all the dressing rooms opened with the same key. One of those swipe cards. It had to be that way because the band and the crew were running in and out, setting things up."

"Do you know when the theft happened?"

"If it was one of the roadies, yeah. Rats and the others went out to lunch with the promoter. Anybody with a key card could have slipped in."

"I'm surprised no one was in charge of guarding the equipment."

Beal sighed. "Well, that's another thing. It was my turn to play watchdog. But remember, this was a hometown gig. My girlfriend showed up and I'd been on the road for months. We found an empty room—"

"You two were getting reacquainted when you were supposed to be keeping the theft from happening. Another reason to suspect you."

"I guess so. Okay, now I have to tell you about the other roadies."

"No, you don't. What you have to do is put on your turn signal and take the next exit. I'm not so drunk that I don't know Route 24 is the fastest way home."

"All right already."

"I'm not paying for a longer trip just so you can fill in extra details."

"Okay. But how can you solve the crime if you don't hear it all?"

"I can't. Nobody can solve a crime, with no physical evidence, no witnesses to interrogate, and only one person's shaky memories to work from." Shanks rubbed his eyes, which felt like he'd been pouring sand into them. "The best anyone can do is give you a theory that fits the facts. I have a theory, so let's throw some facts at it and see if they stick."

"How can you have a theory already?"

"In vino veritas." Great. Now he was throwing out quotations in Latin. "I have three questions."

"Okay. What's your first one?"

Hmm. He'd had it a minute ago. Oh, yes. "After you were fired, did you get another job as a roadie?"

Beal snorted. "I couldn't exactly ask for a reference, could I?"

"I guess not."

"Besides, all the road managers know each other. I was blackboxed. I guess I could have tried one of the small-time bands, but I have my pride, man."

"Of course. So what did you do?"

"Michelle's dad got me a job in construction."

"Michelle?"

"The girlfriend." Another sigh. "That didn't work out."

"Sorry to hear it. Okay. Question two."

"You already asked two."

Shanks' bushy eyebrows dropped in a scowl. "One was a follow-up. Give me some wiggle room here."

"Okay. Go on."

"Your locker where they found the evidence. What kind of lock was on it?"

Beal's eyes went wide. "You kidding me? That was, like, a decade ago. You think I remember the brand?"

"Not the brand. Key or combination?"

"Oh. Let me think. Combination."

"Okay. Was it – This is another follow-up question."

"Yeah, I get it."

"Was the combination installed in the factory or was it one you put in yourself?"

"I used my street address from when I was a kid. In case that matters," he said sarcastically.

"It might. Only because you probably used it elsewhere. Here's the third question. What did what's-her-name, Muriel—"

"Michelle?"

"Right. What did she think of your dream job?"

Beal pondered. "She liked it at first. Thought it was cool, you know? That's how we met. She came to a show and talked her way backstage one night. Man, she was wearing this red tank top—"

"No offense, but we'll run out of highway before you finish that story. I take it Michelle changed her mind about the job?"

"Yeah. When I was on the road for months at a time. And there were the drugs. Plus the fact that Rats was crazy."

And all those girls in tank tops, Shanks thought. "Well, that's it."

"That's what?"

"Your answer. Or at least *my* answer. Your girlfriend stole the cocaine."

Beal stomped his brakes and the taxi jerked to the right. Shanks's head thumped the window. "Be careful!"

"You're out of your freaking mind! She hated drugs."

"I didn't say she *used* the stuff. It was returned untouched, right?"

"Well, yeah. But for God's sake, why would she take it?"

"Because your dream job was her nightmare. She wanted you home where she could keep you safe."

"But Rats could have killed me for that!"

"If he tried she would have moved to Plan B: confessing. Would Rats have killed *her?*"

Beal thought for a moment. "No. If she told him she did it to get me fired he would have probably thought it was funny. He liked it when guys seemed henpecked. Guys other than him."

"So that's my theory." Shanks settled deeper into the seat and closed his eyes.

"Well, it's nuts. If she felt that way— Huh... You know, that might explain..." Beal drifted off into silence, reinterpreting some memories.

"Too bad you don't know where Michelle is. Asking her would be the only way to see if I'm right."

"Oh, I know where she is." Beal didn't sound happy. "I'm married to the manipulative little—"

Shanks eyes popped open. "You told me it didn't work out."

"I meant the job her father got me. The marriage is fine. At least I *thought* it was. Boy, when I get home—"

"Now, hold on." The last thing Shanks wanted was for his name to show up in a divorce proceeding, or something worse.

He thought fast. "You don't seem to realize how lucky you are."

"Damn right I don't!" A pause. "How do you figure?"

Good question. "Well, look. You're married to a woman who was willing to commit a crime, to risk violence, even to protect you from what she saw as danger. Do you realize how rare that type of *passion* is?"

A few blocks passed in silence. "When you say it like that, it's kind of cool."

"And really, how long would a job like that have lasted, anyway?"

"Well. The band broke up a couple of years later. There was a police raid..."

Shanks let out a breath. "You should be grateful."

"Huh. Do you think I should tell her I know?"

"Save it for a special occasion."

"She's got a birthday coming up next month."

"Perfect." Actually, Shanks had meant Beal should use it when he needed to apologize for a screw-up. But whatever worked. "This is my corner."

"Right." The cab turned up the hill. "I gotta thank you, man. You solved a problem that's been driving me nuts for ten years. You sure know a lot about women."

"You exaggerate."

"I'll bet you and your wife have a great relationship. Look! She even stayed up waiting for you."

Shanks looked. Every light on the ground floor was on. That was not good.

He paid with a credit card.

"Hey," said Beal. "You don't have to tip. You already gave me plenty."

"That's okay."

"Well, at least take my business card. Call me next time you need a ride somewhere."

There was a shadow on the living room wall. Cora was pacing back and forth.

"I don't think I'm going to need taxis for a while," said Shanks.

Decades ago my wife and I went to the Capitol Theatre in Passaic, New Jersey to see Randy Newman. It was a great show but we agreed afterwards that we never wanted to go again to such a large, overwhelming theatre.

About a week later the Rolling Stones announced that they were going to tour America, only performing in small, intimate venues. They started, of course, at the Capitol Theatre.

And I guess that is one of many differences between folk and rock.

This story appeared in HITCHCOCK'S in April 2013.

SHANKS HOLDS THE LINE

"Please hang on," said Leopold Longshanks. "I'll have to start up my computer. It's down in the basement."

"Of course," said Jake. "I'll wait."

"You're too kind,' said Shanks. He was in his home office, checking his e-mail. His publisher had replied, in a cranky mood, concerning Shanks' complaint about the proposed cover for his new novel. The artist had apparently been unaware that only the *bullet* is fired out of a gun, not the entire *cartridge*. You would think the publisher would be grateful Shanks caught it before they all got laughed at, but no.

There was also an email from the organizers of a conference, reminding him that he had agreed to speak. Shanks was happy to do so, good publicity, but was less than thrilled by the topic they had assigned him. He was supposed to find something new to say about that old classic: why do people read mysteries?

The question we should be asking is why more people don't. If we could double the readership I could buy a better computer, and a new smartphone—

Phone. He picked it up. "Jake? You still there?"

"Yes, sir." He had a slight accent. East Asian, perhaps?

Jake had called a minute earlier, identifying himself as being "from the technical support division of Windows. We have reports that your computer is sending out malicious messages. Apparently it is infested with malware."

"My gosh," Shanks had said. "That's terrible."

"Yes sir. Your computer could crash at any moment. But I can fix it for you."

"Really? That's wonderful! How can you do that?"

"I have to take control of your computer for a few minutes. Are you in front of it now?"

And so it began.

Frustration. That was the thesis for Shanks' speech. People are drawn to mysteries because they are frustrated by injustice. Crimes unsolved. Felons unpunished.

He had planned to use bankers in the mortgage collapse as a showpiece – nobody in that whole crowd had done anything indictable? – but now he was thinking there might be a better, local example.

Namely Betty Shawcross, right across the street. Nicest neighbor you could ask for, although she was getting up there, close to eighty.

One day, about six months ago, she had come rushing over in tears. Seems she had received a phone call about malware on her computer and let the authority figure on the other end take control of her machine. By the time Shanks and his wife arrived the machine was spitting out its contents to some distant interloper and neither the off button nor CTRL-ALT-Del would stop it. Shanks had had to yank the plug out of the wall.

The computer technician they brought the machine to said flatly that he wasn't going to mess with the infected thing. "Replace it."

But Betty didn't want to.

"How much money did she lose?" Shanks asked later.

"Not much," said Cora. "That wasn't as bad as having to get new credit cards, and change bank accounts. But here's the worst part, Shanks. I told her 'it could have happened to anyone,' and you know what she said? 'It would never have happened to me five years ago. There's no way I would have fallen for that.' Now she's so afraid that she's falling apart that she doesn't want to buy another machine."

"That's terrible," said Shanks. "She's always talking about video-calling her grandkids."

Cora nodded. "Her son is trying to talk her into buying another computer. Boy, I'd like to hurt those creeps."

"Me too, my love. But there's no way to get at them."

"Jake? You still there?"

Amazingly, he was. "Yes sir. Are you ready now?"

"Almost, my friend." Shanks sipped coffee. "Just hang in there."

And here was an email from his Hollywood agent, still trying to get a rational explanation from the studio about the allegedly disappointing net profits on their film.

Talk about felons unpunished.

Speaking of which, the phone was buzzing, signaling that Jake had hung up. Ah well.

Shanks opened a new file and began to type out some thoughts on his speech. He would have to disguise Betty's identity, not that anyone at the conference would know her from Dorothy L. Sayers, but you couldn't be too careful these—

The phone was ringing. Excellent.

"Hello?"

"There was a technical problem, sir. We were cut off." Jake sounded a little grumpy.

"I'm so sorry. All right, my friend. I'm sitting in front of my computer now."

"Very good. I just need you to—"

"Wait, wait, wait. I have one question for you first."

"What is it?"

Shanks raised a bushy eyebrow. "Do you have a beard?"

A longish pause. "A what?"

"A beard."

"Why would you want to know that?"

"I want to form some image of you. It's a simple enough question."

A sigh. "No, I don't have a beard. Now, can we—"

"I'm guessing you use an electric shaver."

"Listen, sir, your computer could break down at any minute. I will not be responsible if—"

"Then don't waste time. Do you—"

"Yes! I use an electric shaver. Why?"

"I thought so," said Shanks. "If I robbed people for a living I wouldn't dare face myself in the mirror every morning with a razor in my hand. Jake? You there?"

Dial tone.

Shanks checked his watch as he hit the off button on the phone.

He had kept Jake from ripping anyone off for a full quarter of an hour.

It was one minute off his personal best. Not to worry; sooner or later one of Jake's friends would call back and give him another chance.

I wrote this story because the mother of a friend of mine suffered a fate very similar to Mrs. Shawcross. The second time I received a call like that – from someone who called himself "Jake" – I decided I wanted to warn the world about it, and suggest to people that they use the tactic illustrated in this story.

So I found myself with a piece of flash fiction (usually defined as under 1000 words; this one is about 950) and I wasn't sure what to do with it. If I sent it to HITCHCOCK'S by the time it was accepted and published (if and if, of course), the scheme might have mutated beyond recognition.

I got an idea. I sent it to Linda Landrigan and told her that if she chose she could put it up at Trace Evidence, the blog for HITCHCOCK'S. I don't write fiction for free, but I have always made an exception for charity, and this seemed to qualify, since I considered it a public service. The story went up on May 5, 2014. This is its first non-blog appearance.

Which brings us to the end of this book.

Will Leopold Longshanks have any more adventures? I hope so. There is another story sitting in the pile on Linda's desk. The odds that she will accept it (based on past performance) appear to be 2 to 1.

I have a notebook full of ideas for him and I hope that some will gel into full adventures. I enjoy the old grump's company.

I also hope you enjoyed these enough to want more. Thanks for your attention.

ABOUT THE AUTHOR

ROBERT LOPRESTI was born in New Jersey. He is a librarian in the Pacific Northwest. More than fifty of his short stories have been published in magazines and anthologies. He has won the Derringer (twice) and Black Orchid Novella Awards, and been nominated for the Anthony Award. His first novel, SUCH A KILLING CRIME, was published by Kearney Street Books in 2005. He blogs regularly at SleuthSayers.com and Little Big Crimes.

Visit the author's website

www.RobLopresti.com

CPSIA information can be obtained
at www.ICGtesting.com
Printed in the USA
LVHW031605260319
611890LV00005B/896/P